More Praise for

# the Season of Styx Malone

An ALA-ALSC Notable Children's Book
A Junior Library Guild Selection

★ "A summertime romp filled with trouble-making,
camaraderie, and substance."
—*School Library Journal*, starred review

★ "A novel that is genuinely funny, heartbreaking,
and uplifting—extraordinary, in fact."
—*Publishers Weekly*, starred review

★ "Spending time with Styx, Caleb, and Bobby Gene is
an experience no reader will soon forget."
—*The Horn Book*, starred review

★ "Reminiscent of now-classic works by Katherine
Paterson, Natalie Babbitt and Lois Lowry . . . brings the
darkness of fear and trauma into the bright sun

Children's Literacy Foundation

clif

This is my book!

clif@clifonline.org ★ www.clifonline.org ★ 802.244.0944

# the Season of
# Styx Malone

## KEKLA MAGOON

A Yearling Book

Text copyright © 2018 by Kekla Magoon
Cover art copyright © 2019 by Charlot Kristensen

All rights reserved. Published in the United States by Yearling, an imprint of Random House Children's Books, a division of Penguin Random House LLC, New York. Originally published in hardcover in the United States by Wendy Lamb Books, an imprint of Random House Children's Books, a division of Penguin Random House LLC, New York, in 2018.

Yearling and the jumping horse design are registered trademarks of Penguin Random House LLC.

Visit us on the Web! rhcbooks.com

Educators and librarians, for a variety of teaching tools, visit us at RHTeachersLibrarians.com

The Library of Congress has cataloged the hardcover edition of this work as follows:
Names: Magoon, Kekla, author.
Title: The summer of Styx Malone / Kekla Magoon.
Description: First edition. | New York : Wendy Lamb Books, [2018] | Summary: Caleb Franklin and his younger brother, Bobby Gene, spend an extraordinary summer with their new, older neighbor, Styx Malone, a foster boy from the city. | Identifiers: LCCN 2017050786 (print) | LCCN 2017060666 (ebook) | ISBN 978-1-5247-1597-7 (ebook) | ISBN 978-1-5247-1595-3 (trade) | ISBN 978-1-5247-1596-0 (lib. bdg.) | Subjects: | CYAC: Adventure and adventurers—Fiction. | Family life—Indiana—Fiction. | Foster children—Fiction. | African Americans—Fiction. | Indiana—Fiction.
Classification: LCC PZ7.M2739 (ebook) | LCC PZ7.M2739 Sum 2018 (print) | DDC [Fic]—dc23

ISBN 978-1-5247-1598-4 (pbk.)

Printed in the United States of America

10 9 8 7 6 5 4 3 2 1

First Yearling Edition 2019

For my cousins:
Anne, Katie, Christopher,
Robin, Michael,
and in memory of David

# CHAPTER 1

## EXTRA-ORDINARY

Styx Malone didn't believe in miracles, but he was one. Until he came along, there was nothing very special about life in Sutton, Indiana.

Styx came to us like magic—the really, really powerful kind. There was no grand puff of smoke or anything, but he appeared as if from nowhere, right in our very own woods.

Maybe we summoned him, like a superhero responding to a beacon in the night.

Maybe we just plain wanted everything he offered. Adventure. Excitement. The biggest trouble we've ever gotten into in our lives, we got into with Styx Malone.

It wasn't Styx's fault, entirely. And usually I'd be quick to blame a mess like this on Bobby Gene, but no matter how you slice it, this one circles back to me.

It all started the moment I broke the cardinal rule of the Franklin household: Leave well enough alone.

+ + +

It was Independence Day, which might have had something to do with it.

I woke up with the sunrise, like usual. Stretched my hands and feet from my top bunk to the ceiling, like usual. I touched each of the familiar pictures taped there: the Grand Canyon, the Milky Way, Victoria Falls, Table Mountain. Then I rolled onto my belly, dropped my face over the side of the upper bunk and blurted out to Bobby Gene, "I don't care what Dad says. I don't want to be ordinary."

"What?" he said.

I knew he was awake. His eyes were open and blinking up at me. He had his covers pushed down and his socks balled up in his fist. He must've heard me.

"I said, I don't want to be ordinary. I want to be . . . the other thing."

"What other thing?" Bobby Gene said.

I rolled onto my back. "Never mind." I didn't really know what I meant, but it was on my mind because of what happened last night at dinnertime.

Dad got home from his shift at the factory around six, which was normal. He turned on the television, piping through the house the sound of news reports about things that were happening so far from here that they barely seemed real. The reporters were always blabbing on about economics and politics and the constant BREAKING NEWS.

But every once in a while I would see something that made me want to reach through the screen and touch it, you know? Like to get closer to it, or to make it a little bit real. There was a story about dolphins one time. And a feature about a group of kids who sailed a boat around the world. Special things. Things you'd never find in Sutton.

The problem was, Dad was always talking about us being ordinary folks—about how ordinary folks like this and ordinary folks need that. He usually said all this to the TV, but our house isn't that big and his voice is pretty loud so you can always hear him.

*Ordinary folks just need to be able to fill the gas tank without it breaking them.*

*Ordinary folks go to church on Sundays.*

*Ordinary folks don't care who you've been stepping out with; just pass the dang laws.*

(A lot of times he said it more colorful than that, but I'm not allowed to repeat that kind of language.)

That night in particular he was getting all hot and bothered, as Mom would say. He was ranting at the TV and Bobby Gene and I were playing Battleship behind the couch. Sneaking back there was a tight fit for us, but we needed to practice undercover operations. Our ongoing spy game was the best thing we'd come up with for summer entertainment thus far.

If I could sink deep enough into the game, it felt like I could take on the whole world. Caleb Franklin, International Man of Mystery. A trench coat, a passport, dark sunglasses and a briefcase of world-saving secrets. An important handoff, code-word clearance—

"Yahtzee!" Bobby Gene yelled. Which was what he yelled whenever he won at anything.

My spy bubble burst. The secret safe house dissolved. My shoulder ached from being squeezed into the couch-wall gap.

I didn't have a passport. I'd never so much as crossed the Sutton town limits.

When the news went to commercial, the ad jingle was a piece of classical music. I popped my head up over the back of the couch. "I know that song. We played it in band. It's 'Tarantelle.'"

"Dinner!" Mom called. Dad turned off the TV.

"Hey," Dad said to me. "You got that from just a few notes?"

I shrugged. "I like that music."

"That's because you're extraordinary," Dad said, patting my shoulder. "Let's eat."

My heart plummeted. I knew Dad thought he was paying me a compliment, since he loves to have ordinary this and ordinary that. Still, my heart sank. Extra-ordinary? Like, so plain and normal that it was something to be proud of?

I hated this. Hated, hated, hated it. Which is why I thought about it all night and into the morning. And why I vowed that, no matter what it took, I was not going to be so ordinary.

✦ ✦ ✦

Dad took us to his union hall that night, for the Fourth of July picnic. Mom had to work, so it was Dad and the three of us kids: Bobby Gene, me, and our little sister, Susie. Susie's only one year old, and Dad wanted to be able to talk to his buddies freely and play cards, so he put Bobby Gene and me in charge of her. That was Dad's first mistake. His second mistake was not forbidding us to play with the fireworks the other boys had brought, the way Mom would have done, and which, of course, was all we wanted to do.

Bobby Gene carried Susie out into the hall's backyard. We weren't concerned about her cramping our style. We could always find some girls to fuss over her and take her off our hands.

But what we found in the backyard was not normal. What we found . . . was mind-blowing.

Cory Cormier stood on one of the picnic tables, alongside the largest gunnysack I had ever seen. It could have

5

held my entire body. Maybe even Bobby Gene's. Everyone—literally every kid in attendance, twenty or thirty of them—was gathered around, shouting and bidding on the goods inside.

"I'll loan you my bike for the week."

"I have twenty allowance dollars coming to me."

"I'll open the back door of the movie theater for you. Twice! Three times?"

I didn't even know what was in the bag, but I began salivating. Bobby Gene said, "What the . . ."

We'd never seen anything like it.

"You'll have to do better than that," Cory chortled from on high. "Maybe I'll have to just sell one to each of you."

"No!" the crowd roared.

Cory reached into the bag and extracted a rocket-style firework the size of his forearm. He held it aloft. "Are you sure?"

The other kids screamed with excitement.

"Let's get in there!" Bobby Gene exclaimed. We were already running.

Never mind that Cory Cormier was one of Bobby Gene's least-favorite people. Never mind that he was known as a big, bad bully who could beat up anyone, anywhere, anytime—and enjoy it. Never mind that a deal struck with Cory would probably have major strings attached.

It was awe-inspiring. Cory was eleven—the same age as

Bobby Gene, and one year older than me. And yet the boy on the table and the bag in his hands loomed larger than life up there.

My mind spun with possibilities.

To be up high. All eyes on me . . .

Yes. I would do whatever it took to become Cory Cormier's right-hand man, doling out fireworks at my whim. I could practically taste the thrill of power.

How would I do it? No idea.

But it turned out not to be so difficult to distinguish myself that night.

As it turned out, Cory Cormier had always wanted a little sister, and we had one to spare.

# CHAPTER 2

## A BAG OF TROUBLE

Here's how it happened. We stood at the edge of the rippling scrum, shouting offers. Anything we could think of. Loans and favors and involuntary servitude.

Suddenly Bobby Gene's face turned sour. He pushed Susie away from his chest in a hurry. "I think she just messed," he said. "I can smell it." He held her aloft with his beefy arms and sniffed.

I tore my eyes from the stage and inspected her red-white-and-blue onesie for any signs of spillover. One thing about babies—they leak. A lot.

"SOLD!" Cory Cormier cried out.

Dang, I missed it!

". . . to Caleb and Bobby Gene Franklin."

What?

Groans of protest swelled out of the crowd. Everyone turned to us.

Bobby Gene lowered Susie so fast that for a second I thought he'd dropped her. She let out a delighted laugh, and up on the stage, Cory Cormier grinned in our direction.

He jumped down, pushed the bag of fireworks at me and stretched his arms out to Susie. She giggled obligingly and banged on his arms with her fat fists.

"That's great, you guys," he said. "Thanks."

I clutched the fireworks to my chest. It was like hugging a bag of cats.

"I always wanted a little sister," Cory said. His words nearly got lost in the jostle of the crowd, which had turned to trying to barter with me now that I had the prize. Being the center of attention felt something like it might feel to be in a pinball machine—as the ball.

A pinball that moves faster and faster and gets more and more power and more and more points. Their energy shot straight into me. *Who's ordinary now?*

"Not for sale!" I shouted. "They're ours."

I would like to say that I didn't entirely understand what I was saying. I'd like to say that, but I can't. Cory scooped Susie out of Bobby Gene's arms. "Whoa," he said. "She's heavier than she looks."

"You're telling me," said Bobby Gene.

We cringed as Cory's bare forearm went around Susie's dirty diaper bottom. "You sure?" he said. She bounced her face against his shoulder, leaving a spit stain, and thrashed her legs. Perfectly happy.

Bobby Gene and I looked at each other. At the burlap sack. At Susie.

"Uh . . . ," Bobby Gene said.

"Uh . . . she needs to be changed," I admitted. The hideous stench wafting up from Susie's backside would surely be a deal-breaker.

"Show me how," Cory said, real serious. "I can do it."

So Bobby Gene ran for the diaper bag while I defended the fireworks and Cory cooed and cuddled our former sister. It seemed like a fair trade, the more I thought about it. One loud, explosive mess for another.

✦ ✦ ✦

Dad was in a tight mood by the end of the evening. This was to be expected. Bobby Gene and I always had more fun at the hall than he did.

Through the sliding door, he called out, "Bobby Gene, Caleb," and then went to wait on the front porch. When we came out, Bobby Gene was carrying the gunnysack, which could easily have been Susie all wrapped up in a blanket or something. Of course, we didn't *come* to the hall with a blanket, but that's the kind of detail Mom would notice, not Dad.

"You ready?" he said.

"Yes, sir."

Dad seemed chill on the surface as he waved goodbye to a few guys on the porch. We knew better. Underneath he was all distracted and angry, his head full of other people's politics and a lot of biting his tongue.

We trailed behind him on the walk home, lugging the gunnysack and trading it off between us, but Dad stared at the ground. Going to the hall was like a job to Dad. A job he hated. *The more they see of us, the more they'll know we're just like them,* he'd say, if we asked, which we didn't anymore. It was his way of keeping us safe, Mom explained, which didn't make a whole lot of sense.

When we got to the house, Dad flipped on the TV. He turned to the channel that told the news the way he liked to hear it. Over his shoulder, he said, "Put Susie in the crib, okay?"

"Uh, sure," we said. Then we ran to our room and examined each and every firework. Soon we heard Mom's car in the driveway.

Bobby Gene and I looked at each other and right about then we both got a real bad feeling in our stomachs. We shoved the rockets into the bag and the bag under the bed and got the edges of Bobby Gene's comforter pulled down just in the nick of time.

Our bedroom door banged open. "WHERE IS YOUR SISTER?"

# CHAPTER 3

## NO TAKE-BACKS

Bobby Gene and I took pains to assure Mom and Dad that Susie was probably perfectly fine and safe over at Cory Cormier's place. We shouldn't have said "probably." Mom's eyes became like two chocolate-brown lasers, slicing through us from our bedroom doorway. Dad stood in the hall behind her. "Unbelievable," he muttered.

"GET in the car," Mom said in a small, tight voice. A voice that meant massive trouble. Her voice had escalated right through shouting mode into a high, quiet dogs-only range.

Just to be perfectly clear: Bobby Gene and I were the dogs in this scenario. We scurried out to Mom's station wagon with our tails between our legs.

✦ ✦ ✦

Mrs. Cormier opened the screen door and immediately pushed Susie into Mom's arms. "I'm so sorry. I was absolutely horrified when Cory came home with her. Of course I would have brought her back over to you right away, but he wouldn't tell me whose she was." She glared over her shoulder. Cory Cormier was seated at the dining room table, head bowed.

"Thank you," Mom said. She kissed Susie's sleepy, slobbery face and held her close. The enormity of our recent stupidity washed over me.

"Come in," Mrs. Cormier said, pushing the screen wider. "All boys, on the couch."

We slunk inside. Cory scooted away from the table and joined us. The couch was a threadbare blue stripey thing, with cushions flattened from long use. I sat on one side, Cory on the other, Bobby Gene in the middle.

Mom and Mrs. Cormier stood in front of us. Double-barrel mom-stare. We were in deep doo-doo. Quicksand-deep.

"Explain yourselves."

"Caleb and Bobby gave her to me," Cory said. "I didn't steal her."

"It was a fair trade," Bobby Gene blurted. Cory Cormier's eyes grew wide and terrified.

Mom glared at us. "Your sister is not a form of currency," she snapped.

"Trade for what?" Mrs. Cormier asked, eyeing us suspiciously.

Cory Cormier's desperate gaze pierced me. I grabbed Bobby Gene's arm. "Cory wanted a sister! He was going to show us some basketball tricks," I said. "And let us share his hoop."

"Instead, the three of you will spend that time doing extra chores together," Mom said.

*Like babysitting?* I wanted to ask, but I didn't think they'd find it funny.

"For the next four weeks," Mrs. Cormier added. But that would be almost the whole rest of our summer vacation.

"One hour a day," said Mom. An hour a day with Cory Cormier? No way!

"Sometimes here and sometimes at the Franklins'," said Mrs. Cormier.

"Plenty of odd jobs to be done," Mom added. "You'll be busy enough."

They spoke in the exact same tone of voice. Mom-mad. Did they plan this somehow, or can they read each other's minds, like they could obviously read ours?

"Do you understand?"

We nodded.

"Franklin boys." Mom whisked a finger in front of us. "Car."

Bobby Gene let out a big breath. Our trial was over. Time

to go home. As we slid toward the door, Cory Cormier shot me a last grateful look. He was almost . . . smiling. I don't know what he had to be so happy about. He was still in the same hot mess that we were.

Then his eyes narrowed. "I'm coming for you," he mouthed.

✦ ✦ ✦

Over breakfast, Mom announced that Cory Cormier would be coming over at ten to do chores with us. "You're going to weed the garden and then you're going to string up the new chicken wire Dad bought to keep the rabbits out."

The chicken wire was not exactly new. It had been leaning up against the side of the house since April. I didn't much mind weeding the garden, usually. Doing it with Cory, well . . . these were the consequences of trying to be unordinary. Like Dad always says, *When you act too big for your britches, the world has a way of slapping you down.*

I leaned over and gave Susie a little coochie-coo under her bib. She squawked and banged her rubber spoon. Applesauce splatter.

"Great," Mom said. "That's perfect, Caleb." She slung the dish towel off her shoulder and wiped at the spots on the table.

I slid into my seat across from Bobby Gene. I knew

enough to keep my mouth shut, even though it wasn't fair for Mom to call me out on that one. Susie would sure enough splatter applesauce whether I did anything or not.

There was a bowl of it on the table for the rest of us too. I spooned a generous helping onto my plate.

Bobby Gene looked pointedly at me over the potato pancakes. He kept stretching his eyes all big and waggling his eyebrows. He was trying to do the thing where we communicated without talking. But it only worked some of the time.

"Later," I mouthed to him.

When the phone rang, Mom retreated to the other side of the kitchen. "Hi, Camille. Yes, send him over anytime."

Bobby Gene leaned in. "Gotta hide them *now*."

# CHAPTER 4

## MEETING STYX MALONE

Cory Cormier was coming. We were on the run. We plowed through the woods, lugging the gunnysack, passing it back and forth between us when it got heavy.

"How far we gonna go with this?" I asked, huffing under the weight of the sack. This was what I got for trying to make myself stand out. I could hear Dad's voice in my head. *You're just like everyone else. Don't let them tell you different.*

Two paces ahead of me, Bobby Gene was walking like he was on a mission. Which, of course, he was.

"We can just stash it here, right?" I said. All we really needed was for the stuff to be out of sight for a little while. "Cory's gonna be at the house any minute."

"We could just keep going," Bobby Gene said, his voice a mix of pathetic and hopeful.

"Yup," I agreed. "And never come back."

This was a switch. Usually I was the one saying we

needed to get out of Sutton and see the world. Bobby Gene always sided with Dad. *We've got everything we need right here, boys.*

But the threat of Cory Cormier was some powerful Kryptonite. *No sudden movements, son. Keep your hands where they can see them.*

"Your turn," I said, pausing my stride. Bobby Gene gave no sign of stopping. "Come on, okay? You know we can't—"

That's when we ran into Styx Malone.

Well, *tripped over* would be more accurate. We didn't even see him.

He was sitting on a stump at the base of a ragged old shagbark hickory. Eyes closed. Nodding to the rhythm, a pair of knobby little buds in his ears. Long legs stuck out in front of him, and right in our path.

Bobby Gene went sprawling. He yelped as he fell, except he never hit the ground.

Styx flew up like his seat was on fire. He grabbed Bobby Gene midsprawl and wrestled him upright. Styx's elbow locked around Bobby Gene's throat. "What gives?" he shouted. "Why you running up on me? I ain't do nothing."

It took me a minute to figure out how to answer. The very last thing we were expecting right then was to see any other person.

Styx clearly felt the same. "What are you doing in my backyard?"

"This is *our* backyard," I said. "Not yours."

This was not remotely true. We had run pretty far beyond our property. But this was public land. Styx had no more claim on the woods than we did.

Styx Malone squeezed Bobby Gene's throat tighter, yanking Bobby Gene back against his chest. His fingers were dark and his nails all smudged with grease. He was a whole head taller than Bobby Gene, but he was scrawny, with long, knobby limbs like a praying mantis. Bobby Gene was built like a box full of bricks. It should've been a fair fight.

Bobby Gene's eyes started bugging out of his head. He reached up and grabbed Styx's narrow wrists. He kicked his feet back, one after the other, trying to cut his captor down at the ankles.

Styx was some kind of ninja. He dodged Bobby Gene's kicks, then swooped his legs forward—both at the same time, however impossible—and looped Bobby Gene's ankles, locking the two of them together like a funky pretzel.

Slickest move I'd ever seen.

Bobby Gene's throat convulsed in silent outrage. He looked like a starfish, with his legs splayed and his elbows flailing.

"What are you doing here?" Styx said, holding firm.

We had a perfectly good explanation, as if we needed one. Yet my only comeback was: "What are *you* doing here?" At this point, I was 0 for 2. And Bobby Gene was no help, seeing as he couldn't breathe, let alone speak.

Between the two of us, Bobby Gene and I had been in our share of fights around the playground, but nothing life-threatening. We always had each other's back. But I already had my hands full. I wasn't about to set the gunnysack aside.

"Stop it!" I said. "You're killing him."

Styx Malone was black like us, only darker. He was darker than anyone I'd ever met. That was one of the things I was thinking, even while he was busy squeezing the life out of my brother.

"Your friend's got about sixty seconds of air left in him," Styx Malone said.

"He's my brother," I said. "Let him go."

I got up the courage to look into Styx's eyes. He had dark eyes. In the shadows, they appeared almost black. But his expression didn't seem mean. He seemed . . . scared.

"We're not going to hurt you," I said.

Even with his bugged-out eyes, Bobby Gene managed to glare at me for saying it. That was when I knew he was going to be okay.

"You can let him go."

"You back up first," Styx said. "And drop the bag."

I carefully set down the large sack and took two steps back. "Okay. It's okay."

Styx's eyes shifted, like he was looking to see who else was with us.

"We're alone. We're running away," I said. "We're in big trouble." Running away? Well, that was stretching the truth. But those were the words that came out of my mouth.

Slowly Styx relaxed his death grip on Bobby Gene. Bobby Gene wrestled free and ran around behind me. If the situation hadn't been so dire, I'd have been laughing at the freaked-out look on his face. Not to mention the fact that he was now hiding behind his little brother. His *baby* brother, as he likes to point out.

"What gives, man?" Bobby Gene panted, the moment he had his breath back. "We never did nothing to you."

"Sorry." Styx shuffled his feet. His lanky arms fell to his sides, harmless. "Where I'm from, when people run up on you, you gotta act quick."

"Shoot first, ask questions later?" Bobby Gene mumbled, rubbing his neck.

"Something like that."

"I think we got off on the wrong foot," I said. I stuck my hand out toward him. "I'm Caleb Franklin and this is my brother, Bobby Gene."

Styx eyed my hand for a while, then he grabbed it and squeezed. The handshake was quick and awkward, like maybe he was new to that sort of pleasantry. "Styx Malone."

"Where do you live?" Bobby Gene asked.

"I don't live here. I'm just staying here," Styx answered.

"Where's that?" I asked.

Styx hitched his chin over his left shoulder. I didn't actually know what was in that direction; I had always assumed more woods.

"You have a house?" Bobby Gene asked. "Where you're staying?"

"Yeah, it's a house," Styx said. "What do I look like? I live in a tree?"

"I didn't mean nothing by it," Bobby Gene mumbled.

"You live by yourself?" I asked.

Styx grinned. "Heck no. I'm a minor. I got plenty of people keeping tabs on me." His smile brightened. My skin turned warm despite the morning breeze.

"What's in the bag?" Styx asked.

I opened my mouth to answer.

"We can't really talk about it," Bobby Gene said. "That's why we're in trouble."

Styx walked right over to the bag.

If it was anyone else, we might have tried to stop him. But he was the only guy we knew who'd ever gotten the drop on Bobby Gene.

"Wow," Styx said. "That's the most awesome collection I've ever seen."

"We know," Bobby Gene said, hanging his head.

"We warned you," I said.

Styx reached into the bag. If it was anyone else, there's no way we would have let him do it. But even though we had only just met, even though he had almost just killed one of us, we knew there was something special about Styx Malone. It's like we could feel his power, like we could sense all the changes he would bring into our lives. So when he stuck his hands into our bag, we didn't try to stop him.

If we had, this wouldn't be the beginning of the story. It would be the end.

# CHAPTER 5

## "ANYTHING MAN"

"Of course, we had to keep Susie," Bobby Gene told Styx Malone. Once he laid eyes on our spoils, we had to explain everything. "But we've got the fireworks still."

"And now we have to get rid of them, before anyone finds out or Cory hunts us down," I added. Bobby Gene glanced over his shoulder, like Cory had followed us.

Styx raised an eyebrow. "The kid who wanted to snuggle your baby sister? That's who you're afraid of?"

Well, when you put it like that . . . Sheesh.

"You don't understand," Bobby Gene said. "Cory Cormier is not someone you want to mess with."

Bobby Gene knew more about Cory than I did, since they were in the same grade. Bottom line: Cory was exactly the kind of boy you'd expect to be caught auctioning off a massive bag of probably stolen fireworks. He ruled the schoolyard like some kind of sixth-grade mob boss.

"Listen, that was a shrewd deal." Styx looked impressed. "You gave up nothing and got something major in return."

Hey, yeah. That was true. My chest and cheeks warmed beneath the glow of Styx's favor.

"Gave up nothing except an hour a day on chores," Bobby Gene grumbled.

"I have to do chores around the house anyway," Styx said. "Don't you?"

"Well, yeah," Bobby Gene said. "But not every day like this."

"And not with Cory Cormier." I tapped my wrist as if I was wearing a watch. "Speaking of which, we have to get back."

Bobby Gene and I both stared at the bag of fireworks. We were supposed to be hiding them from Cory. Instead, we'd wasted time explaining ourselves to Styx Malone.

"I'll take them off your hands," Styx said. "Don't even worry about it. You'll never have to lay eyes on them again." He held out his hand.

Bobby Gene and I glanced at each other. "We give them to you, in exchange for what?" I tucked the bag back behind me.

Styx smiled. "Good. I'm glad you didn't fall for that. There's hope for you yet."

"In exchange for what?" Bobby Gene echoed.

"Actually, I'd like to make you a more attractive offer."

Styx reached into his pocket and extracted two small cards. He handed one to me and one to Bobby Gene. The most surprising thing about it was that those ragged pants he was wearing had any pockets left that would hold anything.

The cards read:

**Styx Malone**
Anything Man

Of course Styx had a business card. He was just that kind of cool.

Bobby Gene looked downright impressed. I was too, but mostly I was noticing how the cards had no contact information on them.

"Let me work with you," Styx said.

"Work with us how?" Bobby Gene asked.

"Sounds to me like you need a mediator."

"A meditator?" Bobby Gene echoed. "How's that new age stuff going to help us?" His tone sounded exactly like Dad's when the yoga class ads came on TV. I snickered.

"No, a me-di-a-tor," Styx repeated, enunciating the syllables. "Like a lawyer, to help the Cormier kid see the error of his ways. I can do that." He said it with such intensity that I could almost see him pounding his fist into his palm.

"We don't want to hurt him." My protest sounded lame.

Styx shrugged. "No need. I'll just help him see that the fireworks are rightfully yours."

Bobby Gene and I exchanged a glance that fell somewhere between "Say what?" and "Heck yeah!"

"You covered for him," Styx went on. "That counts for something. You just have to parlay it into something more."

"Parlay?" Bobby Gene said.

"Negotiate. Make him see the value of what you've already given."

"Sure, sure," I said, although I wasn't sure at all what Styx was talking about.

"Then, when Cormier's out of the way, I'll show you how to get rid of that sack the right way."

"What's that mean?" Bobby Gene asked.

Styx tapped his chin. "We'll sell the fireworks, or trade them for something."

"Like what?" I asked.

"Uh, you don't have time for me to explain now, do you?" Styx said. "He's probably already waiting."

I lifted the fireworks bag again. "Yeah. We have to go."

"What do we do with these?" Bobby Gene looked worried. He lowered his voice to a stage whisper. "We can't leave them with *him*."

Bobby Gene was not known for his subtlety.

Styx, of course, heard everything. "I don't expect you to trust me right off," he said. "Tuck them in the woods, closer to your house. I won't even watch."

"Is that going to work?" Bobby Gene wondered aloud.

Styx's expression turned eloquent. We soon learned that meant he was about to speechify us.

"Look, here's the deal. You stash the sack. In an hour, I'll come mediate your dispute with Cormier. Consider it handled. Then you'll owe me, right? So we'll sell or trade off the fireworks and share the proceeds. The stuff we get in return."

I smiled to myself. Styx had finally realized that vocabulary was not among Bobby Gene's strengths.

"We got a deal?" Styx asked.

I opened my mouth, ready to agree. From minute one, I was all in on Styx Malone.

"Wait, what's the split?" Bobby Gene interjected, proving he wasn't born yesterday.

Styx's shoulder popped up. "Fifty-fifty, I reckon."

"Naw," Bobby Gene answered. "Two of us, one of you. That means thirds." Where he was getting these sudden smarts, I hadn't the foggiest.

"But I'm bringing all the expertise," Styx said. "Would you rather have two-thirds of nothing and a big problem on your hands, or would you rather have fifty percent of a whole lot, problem-free?"

"Uh," Bobby Gene said.

Styx offered a ninjalike smile.

I jumped in. "We could say the same to you. A third of the proceeds from our stash, or fifty percent of nothing?" I was getting the hang of it now. Negotiating felt good.

Styx studied us, hawklike. "Caleb and Bobby Gene Franklin, huh?" He spoke our names slowly, then grinned. "I like how you two operate."

A beat of silence passed.

"Fair enough," Styx said. "We go thirds."

The deal was on the table. Bobby Gene still looked skeptical. But how could we pass it up?

"That's my offer," Styx said. "Take it or leave it."

We took it.

# CHAPTER 6

## CHORES WITH CORY CORMIER

Cory wasn't in the backyard waiting for us like we expected. It was too good to be true that he hadn't showed. This was unlikely to be one of those times when our parents issued a punishment and then forgot to follow through on it. That was for minor transgressions. This was a doozy.

"Mom!" we called, stomping in through the back door. "If Cory doesn't show, does that mean—"

"Hey, guys."

File under "Sights I Never Expected to See": The big, bad Cory Cormier standing in our living room bouncing Susie on his hip. A wide grin on his face.

"Look, she still likes me," he said.

Susie gurgled.

"Uh," said Bobby Gene. That was Susie's spit-up face. Cory was about to get drenched.

I leaped toward the high chair and whipped a loose

cloth diaper off the back of it. I slung it over Cory's chest and shoulder.

*Splat.*

Cory laughed. "Whoa."

Bobby Gene and I gave Cory a pretty wide berth after that. Anyone so delighted by infant spit-up was clearly unbalanced.

"Okay, boys. Hop to it." Mom deployed her drill sergeant voice. "Out into the yard."

We trooped outside and stood awkwardly beneath the morning sun. Cory slid a pair of fierce-looking Harley-Davidson sunglasses on. I swallowed hard. Cory always swore he had an uncle in a motorcycle gang. That was where he learned all his best fight moves.

Cory crossed his thick arms and sneered. "Okay, losers. Let's do this thing."

Bobby Gene got smaller after that. It was like he breathed out all the air in his lungs and forgot to bring in any new.

I narrowed my eyes, trying to make them cut like lasers. Cory had seemed cool and powerful last night, with the fireworks in hand. But in the light of day, behind those stupid shades, he was just a great big bully.

"Okay, baby lover," I snapped.

Cory's mouth thinned. He barely had lips to begin with. His mouth was like a seam in his face. "You're dead, Franklin." He took two steps toward me.

I stood my ground. It was our house. We were in charge. I pulled in air to fill out my chest and tried to remember the lessons Bobby Gene had given me about when and how to throw the first punch.

"Guys." Bobby Gene's voice was small. "Let's just do the work, okay?"

"Over here." I stomped past both of them. If Cory wanted to start things off with insults, someone had to show him we couldn't be pushed around.

We led Cory toward the side of the house and dragged the cylinders of chicken wire toward the garden.

Next we headed for the toolshed. Bobby Gene levered the door open.

"Ew," Cory said.

The musty, earthy smell in there was familiar to me. But Cory plugged his nose like one of us had just taken a dump in front of him.

We pulled out all the gardening equipment that seemed useful for weeding and fence construction. Our spades, the big shovel, the hoe, and a crate to put the weeds in. Bobby Gene grabbed the hedge clippers, which he was allowed to use but I wasn't. We didn't even really need them. He probably just grabbed them to make himself look tougher.

We also dragged out Dad's C-3PO stepladder, which we definitely didn't need, but it just looked cool. Even Cory thought so. I could tell because he didn't say something mean about it. We set it up along the edge of the garden plot and took turns climbing up it to "supervise" the weeding.

We stuck out our fists. Bobby Gene counted it out. "One, two, three, shoot."

Paper beat rock beat rock, so Bobby Gene got first watch. He climbed up the ladder, which was taller than any of us, while Cory and I crawled into the garden.

"Oooh," Cory said. "You have a lot of clay."

"So what?" I snapped.

Cory shifted his eyes. "I was just saying."

"Maybe you should stop just saying."

We did have a lot of clay. Every spring, Mom had us dumping layers of bagged soil and manure on top of the garden plot to help the seeds along. The things we grew best were pretty hardy: tomatoes, squash and carrots. Lots and lots of carrots. Luckily the vegetables had all grown tall enough that we could easily tell what was weeds and what wasn't.

Mom was growing three rows of tomatoes right in the center of the garden. She planted tomatoes called Big Boy for Bobby Gene, Morning Glory for me and Early Girl for Susie. Who knew there were this many varieties of tomato? If it was up to me there would only be two kinds: the normal size and the cherry size.

Bobby Gene used my spy binoculars to study our progress from on high. "You missed one over on the left," he instructed as I finished the first row.

I pulled the offending weed, then brushed my hands off. "Trade!" I ordered.

Bobby Gene climbed down and handed over the binocs.

Yes. The magnification was pretty good. From up here I could see detail down to the whorl of brown hair on top of Cory's head. His longish hair flopped into his eyes and he pushed it back from time to time. I couldn't quite imagine what that would feel like. Our hair only grew up and out.

Mom always planted a row of corn even though that was a bit of a fool's errand. Farmers had corn growing in fields and fields around here, but for some reason trying to grow one small row of it never worked out.

"These are nowhere near knee-high," Bobby Gene said, wading into the corn. "I don't even know if weeding can save them."

"Agree," I said. "But here we are."

"Corn is supposed to be knee-high by the Fourth of July," Cory said from somewhere within the tomatoes. "They're totally not on pace."

"We just said that," I snapped. "You don't have to rub it in."

Cory was wider than me and even wider than Bobby Gene. He couldn't squeeze in between the vegetable rows so well. He was going to crush all Mom's tomatoes.

"Trade," I said, and climbed down. I took Cory's place in the middle of things.

"These are quality," Cory said a moment later, looking through my binocs. "If you zoom in close enough, you can't even tell how lame this garden is."

That was it. The last straw.

"What's your problem? You wanna throw down?" I stood up to fight but tripped on a tomato cage. My feet seemed to be everywhere but underneath me. I skittered and scrabbled, trying to stay upright. No such luck. I landed knee and elbow first in the pile of chicken wire.

I couldn't find my balance. I tumbled tush over tailbone into the grass. Blinking into the cloudless sky, I recognized laughter echoing around me. Bobby Gene and Cory were busting a gut.

But I wasn't done yet. "Come at me. Come at me!" I shouted, even though the main fight at the moment was between my shoelaces and the chicken wire.

"That—" Cory gasped between laughs. "That was the most awesomely messed-up almost-throwdown I've ever seen."

Bobby Gene was trying and failing to keep it together himself. "Dude," he choked out. "Epic."

I brushed myself off and tried to shake some dignity back into my limbs. "Let's go," I croaked. My voice cracked worse than Bobby Gene's ever had.

They howled at me. It was actually funny, how hard they were laughing. I found myself joining in.

Styx once told us that laughter was a magic all its own. I don't remember when or why he said it, but it was a Styx truth if ever there was one. While we were laughing together by the side of the garden, Cory Cormier reached down and freed my shoelace from the grip of the chicken wire.

When he straightened up he was smiling, and so was I. He slid his shades up on top of his head and looked me in the eye.

"Thanks," I said.

"Whatever." Then he added, "You guys are okay, I guess." And that was how we accidentally got rid of Jerk Cory once and for all.

# CHAPTER 7

## MEDIATION

We dug a narrow trench to bury the chicken wire. Bobby Gene drew the line with the hoe and Cory and I followed with trowels, digging it deeper. Cory was slow about it. I had finished my whole side before he was halfway done with his. He had a rock in his hand, turning it over and studying it.

"What are you doing?" I asked.

"Checking to see if it's a fossil."

"Oh, cool."

So that became the game then.

"Rock!" I called out the next time I found something bigger than a pebble. We paused to examine it.

Cory deemed my find "interesting." It pretty much looked like a regular rock to me.

"Is it a fossil? How can you even tell?"

"It would have white lines on it, or some pattern of

stains or grooves. The rock itself could have formed from a bone or bone fragment. I have a book at home that shows some pictures. You can see it when you come over." Cory clenched the rock tighter and looked away. His voice got quieter. "I mean, if you want to."

I shrugged. "Sure."

"So, we could find dinosaur bones?" Bobby Gene peered over our shoulders, casting a nice cool shadow.

"Maybe," Cory said. He opened his fist again.

"That would be awesome." It wasn't hard to imagine that the rock in Cory's palm was once a bone. Maybe a wing bone. From a pterodactyl.

"It's more likely there could be mastodons buried around here," Cory said. "You know, a lot of prehistoric beasts got run over when the glaciers came down."

Bobby Gene frowned. "Wait, didn't the glaciers move like an inch in a millennium? Or something?"

"Yeah," I agreed. "That's why they call it 'glacier pace.' Like how Bobby Gene runs."

Cory snorted. Bobby Gene smacked me on the back of my head. I grinned. "Don't start unless you think you can outrun me."

Bobby Gene's cheeks purpled. "Shut up."

"I guess," Cory said, looking at the fossil. "But I think the mastodons died and their bodies got run over, and then frozen and preserved in ice."

It turned out Cory knew a lot about the ice age. The real ice age. Not the Ice Age movies, which Bobby Gene and I had seen. Cory's interest in archaeology made him seem more special. We had lots of books in our house, sure enough, but nothing I could straight-up quote like Cory was doing.

I liked flipping through the pages in *The KnowHow Book of Spycraft,* and I could remember some of what I'd read, but mostly it was fun to imagine doing important secret work in a faraway place.

"See, look at these lines," Cory said. "Doesn't it remind you of the fossils on display at the Children's Museum in Indy?"

"Oh, yeah, yeah. Totally," I rushed to say, before Bobby Gene could let slip the terrible truth: We weren't allowed to go to the museum. On school field trip day, Bobby Gene and I stayed home.

Bobby Gene stared at me for a long second, then resumed his digging. The last thing we needed was to give Cory any new reason to mock us.

We collected several interesting rocks. Cory catalogued each of them and rated the likelihood of each one being a fossil. It was fun. Hanging with Cory stopped seeming weird and started feeling normal.

"So where are they?" Cory said finally.

My stomach sank. I looked toward the woods. Where was Styx Malone when you needed him?

"I gave Susie back," Cory said. "What gives?"

"Oh, come on," Bobby Gene said. "Did you really think you were going to get to keep her?"

"Then I guess I just *loaned* you my fireworks."

"It seemed like you wanted us to keep them," I said. "We could've brought them back last night."

"But our mom confiscated them," Bobby Gene lied. "We got in pretty big trouble."

Whoa. The king of honesty? Fibbing to cover our tracks? That was a new development.

"That's bull," Cory said. "You never told her jack."

"Yeah-huh." Bobby Gene's bluffing skills were right up there with his vocabulary.

"Nuh-uh. You covered for me," Cory continued.

"Yeah, we did," I said. "So you owe us."

Cory crossed his arms and glowered at us. His eyebrows did a fair bit of talking.

There was no point in getting into this debate now. Styx was coming to mediate.

"Those fireworks are ours now, fair and square," Bobby Gene said.

I wasn't sure that was right. We'd made an agreement and couldn't follow through. But then again, Cory was even dumber than we were, trading for something there was no way he was going to get to keep.

We finished the weeding and planted the chicken wire. Styx ambled up while we were putting the tools away.

"Hello, boys." He drew out the words like a Southerner.

Cory turned wary. "Who's that?"

"Styx Malone. Pleasure to make your acquaintance."

Cory stared at Styx's outstretched hand like he didn't want to touch it. "Is he your cousin or something?" he asked us.

Styx raised his eyebrows. "No relation," he said. "Neighbor, friend, mediator." He handed Cory his card. "I've come to discuss the matter of the gunnysack."

"You told him?" Cory exclaimed.

"Your trade went belly-up and so you're looking for your payday, am I right?"

"I want my stuff back," Cory said.

"But you don't, though. Right? Yesterday, you wanted to trade it."

"Well, yeah, but—"

"What if we can offer you something different in exchange?"

"Like what?"

"First things first. Where'd you get them?" Styx asked.

Cory's eyes shifted. "I'm not at liberty to say."

"Then we're not at liberty to say what happened to them," Bobby Gene retorted.

"Fellas." Styx's voice slid easy into the middle of us. Without even saying more, he caught all of our attention. "What that tells me is the goods are hot."

Cory stood silent.

"Yeah, you don't want them back," Styx said. "You want them gone. We can make that happen."

"In exchange for what?"

Styx's grin spread like soft butter. "Free of charge. You don't have to give us a thing."

"Wait." Cory looked confused. "No, I meant what will you give me?"

"Peace of mind, my brother. You can sleep tonight knowing your mess is someone else's problem."

Styx knew how to paint a picture, but Cory was a tough customer. "That's not fair."

"Peace of mind . . . and a cut of the proceeds." Styx worked fast. "I bet we can get you fifty bucks, easy."

That was a fortune. Cory's eyes lit up. But he was still wary.

"You got a better idea?" Styx said. "Think you can get yourself fifty bucks any other way?"

"Uh, not really, but—"

"Then it's a deal. The Franklins and I will take care of

it." Styx nodded toward us. "I'll pencil you in for noon on Thursday."

I took note when he said businessy things like that.

"Okay," I said. "We'll take care of it then."

"So, it's settled?" Styx announced it, not really asking.

Cory got right up in our faces. "When you win by cheating, it always comes back to bite you."

Styx grinned. "Well, that was downright philosophical." He leaned over Cory's shoulder. "We'll take our chances. Right, boys?"

We never could say no to Styx Malone.

# CHAPTER 8

## THE GREAT ESCALATOR TRADE

On Thursday at noon, we met Styx Malone in the woods behind our house. We found him leaning against the same shagbark hickory tree under which we'd met him. By the time the summer was out we'd be thinking of it as Styx's office.

I wanted to kick back against a tree and just *be*. Styx made it look so easy.

"Well, if it isn't Caleb and Bobby Gene Franklin," he said, as if we had just happened by. He pushed off the trunk and ambled toward us.

His arms hung lanky by his sides. I shook out my shoulders to relax them, like his.

"How's it going with Cormier?" Styx asked. "He giving you any more trouble?"

"Not so far," I said. "He's ready for a payday for sure."

"You've got something good going here," Styx said. "Let's step it up a notch."

"You mean, like, us together?" Bobby Gene asked.

"Sure." Styx shrugged. "The deal was for me to help you." He gripped a low horizontal branch, then swung himself around it like a hinge.

"You really think we can sell all these fireworks?" Bobby Gene's questions were bringing me down. It was easy to believe everything Styx promised, until you started trying to think it through.

"Not only can we sell them, we can sell them all at once." Styx leaned over the branch. His scrawny stomach bowed right over it and his sharp black elbows pointed down toward us like punctuation marks.

"Listen," he said. "I'm going to tell you how it is."

We listened. How could we not? Before meeting Styx, our best story was about the time Bo Hopkins, the Pacers' power forward, rode through town on his way to some charity event. All us neighborhood kids lined up along the side of the street to wave to him. We thought it was going to be like a parade. When his car blew by we waved and all, but he never rolled down the tinted windows, so all we saw was limo. But his license plate said BO HOP, which we did get a pretty good look at, and it had remained at the top of our coolness index right up until today.

"This is how it is," Styx continued. "People have stuff. Sometimes they have stuff that you want. So you gotta take it."

"That's stealing," Bobby Gene said.

Styx shrugged. "I'm not trying to teach you morality. I'm telling you how it is."

"We don't steal," I said.

"You're currently stealing my thunder," Styx said. "I'm trying to tell you how it is."

"Sorry."

We waited. We listened.

"You don't have to steal to get stuff free, you know," he said finally. "You just gotta learn how to make people give you things."

Well, that sounded nice enough.

"You ever hear about the guy who turned a paper clip into a house?"

We hadn't. So Styx spun us a fabulous yarn. It went like this:

✦ ✦ ✦

Once there was a guy who wanted to see how much he could get in exchange for nothing. So he asked a friend if he could have a paper clip. The friend gave him the paper clip for free, because it wasn't worth much. No big deal, right?

Then the guy took the paper clip and went to a different friend. He asked that friend if he'd be willing to trade him a cheap ballpoint pen in exchange for the paper clip.

Now, a ballpoint pen is slightly more valuable than a paper clip, but it's still not worth very much money in the grand scheme of things. So the friend agreed.

The guy kept doing this. He took the cheap ballpoint pen and traded it for a roll of Scotch tape. And then a pair of scissors. And then a stapler. He climbed his way through small office supplies until he was trading a paper shredder for a laser printer.

Thus, the concept of the Great Escalator Trade was born.

The guy took his laser printer and started exchanging for other kinds of electronics, until he traded his way into a brand-new laptop computer. Every trade he made was for something of approximately equal value—it wasn't very unfair to any of the individuals he was trading with. But all along he was trading for something worth slightly more than the last thing.

It took a long time, but eventually he traded the laptop until he got a fancy sound system. Then he traded that for a used car, for a boat, for a newer car, and so on. Eventually he was able to trade a big, fancy yacht for a mansion. And all because one day, years before, he'd asked a friend for a paper clip.

Thus, he proved the Great Escalator Trade was possible. And profitable. Then he lived happily ever after in his mansion.

When Styx finished the story, Bobby Gene and I stood slack-jawed. My imagination lit up like a Christmas tree, glowing with all the possibilities.

"An escalator trade is pretty simple," Styx assured us. "You just have to figure out what you want that's worth all the trouble."

*Not to be ordinary,* I thought. *To see the world.* But Styx was talking about the sort of stuff you could buy.

"Something big," Styx said. "What's the dream, you know? What do you want?"

Truth be told, there were plenty of things we wanted. The really big Super Soakers. Better spy equipment. The life-sized LEGO castle. A trip to Mars. A PlayStation.

"Bigger squirt guns," Bobby Gene suggested. He and I were on the same page, sort of.

"It's gotta be better than the fireworks, though," I said. "Right?"

Styx nodded.

"Unlimited LEGO pieces for life?" Occasionally Bobby Gene showed signs of true vision.

"Better," Styx said. "But maybe even bigger."

Bobby Gene and I exchanged a glance. "We know," we blurted. Simultaneously.

Styx raised an eyebrow. "Yeah?"

"A swimming pool!" Bobby Gene exclaimed. "For our backyard."

Styx stroked his chin. "Hmm. That's a good one. It actually might be too big, though. Hard to hide a swimming pool."

"We don't want to hide it. We want to use it," Bobby Gene argued.

I nudged him. "He means from Mom and Dad, you goof."

"Yeah," Styx said. "The day a giant swimming pool shows up in your backyard, suddenly you've got a lot of explaining to do."

"I guess," said Bobby Gene.

"It's also hard to take care of a swimming pool," Styx said. "Did you know that?"

I nodded. "That's what Dad always says. Too much work and too expensive."

"Your father's a very practical man. No, we need something stealthier than a pool."

We thought about it for a time.

"I've got an idea," Styx said finally. "If you're willing to entertain suggestions."

"Oh, sure." I cocked my head casually. "We can entertain that."

"I'd rather show you than tell you," Styx said. "You know, like a presentation. Real professional."

Bobby Gene and I glanced at each other. Why not?

"It's not far," Styx said. "You game?" He pushed off the branch and kept moving, as if our following was a foregone conclusion.

Bobby Gene grabbed my arm and whispered, "We have to tell Mom if we're leaving the yard."

"Only if we're by ourselves," I argued. "We're with Styx." That was iffy logic, but Bobby Gene didn't fight me on it. "We're way past the yard now anyway," I said. Sure enough, we were already walking, stretching ourselves to keep pace with Styx's long-legged stride.

Nothing could've stopped me from following Styx. If we pulled off a successful escalator trade of our own, we'd be famous for sure. Beyond famous. We'd be epic. Legendary. We'd leave ordinary in our dust.

# CHAPTER 9

## THE GRASSHOPPER

"Not far" to Styx meant walking all the way downtown.

"Where are we going?" Bobby Gene asked for about the dozenth time. We were long past the point of no return. We were definitely supposed to tell Mom before we went this far.

"Lemme show you," Styx said. "Like I said, coolest thing ever."

The familiar route felt brand-new with Styx along. I studied him closely. The way he moved, sliding through the world like the air around him was greased. The way he talked, like everything he wanted was a foregone conclusion. The way he thought all things were possible; it was only a matter of planning, and time.

He came from somewhere outside the small world Bobby Gene and I occupied. When we were with him, I could almost touch that place too. Styx made me hungry for something I didn't know how to name.

We walked along Vine Street, past a bunch of downtown houses, the gas station, the funeral home, the dentist's office, and the bold, blocky sign that said RAND MCNALLY, CPA.

"Not the atlas guy," Bobby Gene and I said in unison as we passed, like we always did. We slapped the corners of his sign for good luck, like we always did.

Styx looked at us funny, which was a little embarrassing, but there was no way around our traditions. Mom kept a Rand McNally road atlas in the back of her car seat, so we had to stare at it anytime we drove anywhere.

We turned on Main and strolled past the scoop shop, the diner, the post office, the bookstore, the record-shop-turned-CD-shop-turned-vintage-everything-shop. The sign still read COSMO VINYL, but the only things vinyl inside were a couple of red-topped barstools and some glued-down records decorating the walls.

"Here." Styx stopped in front of Neville's, the hardware store. His voice hushed reverently. "Behold."

All my air caught in my lungs. Bobby Gene blew out an awe-filled breath.

Behind the big glass windows, on a narrow wooden stage, stood the prize to end all prizes.

It looked like a giant grasshopper. Green head, thorax,

abdomen. Crisp candy shell, handlebars feeling outward like antennae. Red, gold and violet flames shot out from the sides of the engine, slicked back in paint along the thorax. A giant grasshopper with fire powers.

Gold letters embossed on the abdomen read S375-681W.

"Holy . . . ," Bobby Gene whispered.

". . . Moly," I finished.

The moped shined on its pedestal. Glowing like a beacon, especially compared to the display of paint cans on one side and gardening tools on the other. It was too glorious for its surroundings, a truly un-ordinary sight.

Styx Malone laid his hand on the glass, like a prophet. "The S375 is as good as it gets. This, my friends, is the stuff of legends."

I pictured myself zooming up a long, striped ramp, soaring through a circle of flames. Bouncing to a finish surrounded by the cheers of a massive crowd.

"Oh, yeah," I said. "It's—"

"What are we supposed to do with that?" Bobby Gene asked. His practicality was cramping our style.

Styx said, "Ride like the wind."

✦ ✦ ✦

"Let's take a closer look," Styx said. The door chimes tinkled as we trooped inside. The guy behind the counter glanced up from stacking lightbulbs. He nodded to us like we were old friends, then resumed stacking.

The flaming grasshopper was even more attractive without the glass glare blocking our view.

"This is gonna be ours," Styx told us, patting the moped's black seat. "Stick with me and you'll see."

"I don't know," Bobby Gene said. "What would we ever do with a moped?"

"Haven't you ever wanted to ride with the wind in your hair?" Styx asked.

None of the three of us had much hair. Mom kept us shorn pretty tight, and Styx had edges so sharp they could cut like razors. But that didn't matter.

"Yeah," I said, imagining riding with the wind against my scalp. Imagining us going, going, gone. Beyond Sutton, to Indy, Chicago and the great Wild West, on a road that stretched a thousand miles. A smooth glide into infinity.

The moped's green paint gleamed and the flames' gold accents sparkled with splashes of sunshine. It promised power, freedom, speed, adventure ... all for the low, low price of $499.95.

My fantasy clunked to a halt.

"Where are we going to get four hundred and ninety-nine dollars?" Bobby Gene asked.

"And ninety-five cents," I added. "Plus tax."

"Simple. We trade the fireworks for the moped." Styx made it sound real easy.

"Are they worth that much?" I asked.

Styx smoothed the handlebars. "Close enough to trade into it. Trust me."

Our very own Great Escalator Trade. Amazing.

"You can't just trade for stuff in a real store," Bobby Gene said.

"We can trade for this," Styx assured us. "You think a hardware store sells mopeds on the level?"

"Yeah, what's it doing here?" I asked.

"It belonged to the owner's son." The clerk's voice reached us from all the way across the store. "But he's got himself a Harley now."

"Too bad we can't drive," Bobby Gene said.

"I can," Styx assured us. "I'm sixteen. I've got a license."

"Whoa," I said.

Styx shrugged a shoulder. "The last place I stayed, they had a car they let me use sometimes."

"Where was that?" Bobby Gene asked. Styx, of course, didn't answer.

✦ ✦ ✦

We wandered back toward home, two of us feeling a bit shell-shocked. We stepped easy, riffing with Styx about our new plan.

I felt lighter, but stronger. Overshadowed by Styx, for sure, but in his presence, all things felt possible.

Bobby Gene couldn't stop grinning. He stopped harping on how long it would take to get home.

We were smooth. As if we could already taste the glory that the Grasshopper would bring, once it was ours. It was the middle of the afternoon. We were way out of bounds and technically delinquent.

It felt amazing.

# CHAPTER 10

## CANDY CIGARETTES

*Where would we go? How fast could we ride?* The next day, questions about the moped skimmed through my brain like a deck of shuffling cards. I struggled to stay as chill as Styx.

Styx brought us candy cigarettes from someplace. They came in a small box with old-fashioned pictures on it. A broad-smiling white man with his hair all slicked away from a distinct side part. JUST LIKE DAD'S! read the label under his square chin.

"I didn't know they made these anymore," Bobby Gene said.

"I know a guy," Styx said.

Of course Styx knew a guy. That was exactly the kind of cool-as-heck thing that Styx would say.

We were sitting in the grass on the rise at the edge of the school playground. This was within our radius. Usually, Bobby Gene and I would be running up and down the slide or something. But Styx thought it was fun to just hang. So we stared out over the lonely playground equipment, discussing business.

"How long till it's ours?" I blurted out.

"Patience, grasshopper," Styx said.

I grinned at the double meaning. I'd told them about my vision of the moped as a flaming grasshopper.

"If we're gonna do this, we're gonna do it right," Styx said.

Patience was not really my strong suit.

"I figured out what to do with the fireworks," Styx added. "Found a guy we can unload them on."

"Yeah?" Bobby Gene said. "Who?" Sutton wasn't exactly a big town. We might know the guy too.

"I'll show you. We'll go over there tomorrow morning."

"We can't in the morning," I said.

"We've got chores," Bobby Gene added. "With Cory."

"We're still paying off the fireworks," I reminded Styx.

Styx toyed with the cigarette between his fingers. Bobby Gene's was half gone already, crunched up between his teeth. Mine was turning needle-sharp against my tongue, like a candy cane. Someday maybe I'd figure out how to suck it down evenly.

Styx twirled the candy cigarette over his knuckles. "Your old lady's really keeping the jam on you, eh?"

"Yeah, man," I said, leaning back and kicking out my

legs. My elbows landed in the soft grass with a jolt and the cigarette broke in half in my mouth. I pinched the clean end tight with my lips to keep it from falling and clamped my tongue against the roof of my mouth to keep from choking on the pointy end.

"So we'll go in the afternoon, then." Styx appeared to be studying the head of a clover. He didn't notice my flopping around. Bobby Gene noticed, but he didn't say anything to call me out.

"Where will we go first?" I mused aloud.

"Where do you want to go?" Styx said.

"How far can we ride?"

"As far as we want. All the way to the horizon."

I imagined us zipping across the California sand and planting our toes in the ocean.

"No, really," Bobby Gene said.

"Can we go as far as Indy?" I said.

Styx laughed. "Indy?"

My mind flashed to the Children's Museum. Even the most ordinary kids in school got to go there. According to the pictures, there was a dinosaur climbing up the outside of the building. That, I'd like to see for myself.

Styx shook his head. "You want to stay in our own backyard?"

"We haven't been to Indy much," I admitted.

"Much?" Bobby Gene said. "We never leave Sutton."

True. Embarrassing, but true.

Styx tapped his candy cig against his lips. "Why's that?"

"Dad." Bobby Gene and I spoke in unison. He sounded matter-of-fact. Me, fiercer than I meant to. When Dad stopped signing our field trip permission slips, he stopped a lot of other things too. We hadn't left town since I was a baby. I barely remembered it.

*The world is a dangerous place. We're safe here. People know us.*

Styx nodded. "Easy. I'll get you to Indy and show you the sights. That's a promise."

Bobby Gene fidgeted nervously. My whole chest warmed and expanded, too full of . . . something.

Styx plucked a clover blossom from the grass. The round whitish-brown bud seemed to wilt as he lifted it, but that was just how they always looked.

"Granddad says you can eat those," I told him. Styx might have all the big-city knowledge, but I knew all kinds of stuff about small, stupid plants.

"Mom says we shouldn't," Bobby Gene added. "They spray the grounds with pesticides and stuff."

"Huh," Styx said. He popped it into his mouth. "What the heck, right?"

"Oh, yeah," I said, casual as anything. "We can tell you anything you want to know about the local fauna." That sounded impressive, I thought. Local fauna.

"Flora," Styx said absently, twirling another clover stem.

"What?"

"Plants are flora. Fauna is animals."

"We can tell you about both." Bobby Gene's words almost covered the clunking sound of me being an idiot.

"We once saw a squirrel do a backflip from those power lines into that maple tree." I nodded toward the place where it had happened. Styx's brow went up.

"Sure did," Bobby Gene agreed.

"Circus fauna," I joked.

Styx cracked a smile.

"He ended by cruising down the slide," I added. That part wasn't true, but Styx was smiling.

"Spread-eagle," Bobby Gene confirmed. Sometimes we were totally in sync. A well-oiled machine of total bull-hockey, like when we had to cover for each other with Mom. I would have smiled at Bobby Gene, but not in front of Styx. We exchanged a glance. Bobby Gene wasn't smiling either. He knew.

"You'd be surprised how much there is to do around here," I continued.

Bobby Gene nodded sagely. "We used to have snail races."

Styx gnawed on his candy cigarette. "How'd that go, exactly?"

"Damn slowly," I said.

"We haven't checked on them in a while, come to think." Bobby Gene made like he was gonna get up and go somewhere. "I wonder who's winning?"

Styx cracked up. If you'd asked me a day or two before then, what the best feeling in the world might be, I wouldn't have known to say it: making Styx Malone laugh.

# CHAPTER 11

## POLENTA

"Styx Malone, huh?" Mom said. She stood at the stove stirring tomato sauce around chicken meatballs.

"Yeah," I said. "He's the greatest." We'd been going on about him for a while. Leaving out some specifics, of course.

Bobby Gene and I hovered around the stove like pigeons waiting for bread crumbs. She always made three tiny meatballs with the last dab of the meat. They cooked faster than the rest and she would let us spoon out one each. The last one was for her, supposedly, but we never saw her eat it. It was always there one second and then gone the next. Mom, the kitchen ninja.

Mom rolled meatballs over with the spatula. They smelled so good, I leaned into the garlic-and-herb-laced steam. Mom eased me back with her stirring elbow.

"An older boy?" Her voice was a little spicy, like the sauce. "How much older?"

"Sixteen," Bobby Gene said. "And he's been *everywhere.*"

"Mmm-hmmm." Mom nudged him out of the way too.

On the back burner, a pan of polenta simmered and popped. Tiny yellow volcanic bursts.

"He's been all over Indy," I told her. "Even to the Children's Museum." It was never too early to start a campaign.

Mom shot me her trademark "hush up" look. Maybe because Dad strolled into the kitchen right then. But my brain doesn't always work so well when I'm hungry.

"If we went into the city, Styx could show us around," I said.

"No sons of mine have cause to go into the city." The fridge clanked open as Dad reached in for a can of pop.

Bobby Gene shot me a warning glance. I swallowed my next words, whatever they would have been. Choked them down so hard my throat hurt.

Dad returned to the living room.

"Okay," Mom said. "Get your spoons."

We greedily scooped the littles out of the pan and blew on them.

"Good," we declared.

When I looked back, sure enough, Mom's tiny meatball had disappeared too.

"How much longer?" Bobby Gene asked. His stomach was probably growling in earnest now, like mine. The tiny meatball was a tease.

"One of you can whisk the polenta," Mom said. "The other can put out bowls. The wide ones, okay?"

I went for the cabinet and Bobby Gene took up the whisk.

"Oh, honey. Not quite so much butter," Mom chided. Bobby Gene had dumped a whole stick into the polenta and was trying to whisk it in.

"More butter is better!" I chirped in a fakey voice as I lined up the bowls on the counter. That's what Grandma Noonie always used to say. Mom smiled at me over her shoulder, her eyes full of love and sadness and the whole world all at once.

Bobby Gene stabbed at the butter with the whisk. "See, it's melting," he said. "It'll be fine." As soon as he took the pan off the heat, the polenta started to firm up.

Mom leaned over and stretched to kiss him on the forehead. He was almost as tall as her now. Whoa. That was weird.

Me, she could still kiss on the top of my head without stretching. She wrapped her spatula arm around me, squeezing and planting a wet one on my hairline.

"Gross, Mom."

She laughed.

Bobby Gene brought over the polenta. "Go get your father," she told him.

When we were alone, the throat-burning words tumbled

out of me. "Why is he like this?" I opened the silverware drawer so I wouldn't have to look Mom in the eye.

"He's doing what he thinks is best for our family. It's our job to keep you both safe." Mom paused. "In a world where that isn't always a given."

"It's Sutton," I said. "What's going to happen?"

"Sweet boy." Mom smoothed her hand over my hair. "There are a lot of angry people out there."

I folded my arms. "Dad watches too much news."

"That's true."

The silverware clattered from my fingers to the bowls. "Styx isn't like that," I whispered to the forks. "Everything's different for him."

Mom took me by the chin. "Listen to me, Caleb," she said, her voice as creamy as the hot polenta. "I wanna meet this Styx Malone."

# CHAPTER 12

## PIGGY BANKS

Bobby Gene and I pulled our piggy banks from their side-by-side spots on top of our bookcase. I shook mine to listen to its satisfying rattle.

My pig was green and Bobby Gene's was blue. Mine had a little yellow polka-dotted bow tie, and his had a red news-boy hat. They were ceramic, like kitchen mugs, and not too heavy. Unfortunately.

We didn't have much need to spend our savings, so that's why we had never cracked them open before. For all we knew, we were already sitting on hundreds. Maybe thousands.

We set the pigs down on the carpet in front of us and gave them each a last look.

"Goodbye, old friends," I whispered.

"Are we sure we want to do this?" Bobby Gene asked. He

had the hammer in his hand. "I mean, this cash is probably supposed to go for stuff we really need someday."

We needed that moped.

"We have to count it," I said. "Styx will be impressed if we get a head start on the Grasshopper fund."

We'd decided to use this as the moped's official code name in case anyone overheard us talking about it.

"Okay." Bobby Gene still looked skeptical. "So, I really have to hit them with the hammer? It's going to get shards all over the place."

I reached up to his bed and yanked his pillowcase off.

"Here, do it on this." I laid the pillowcase over the carpet like a drop cloth.

"Hey," he complained.

"This is how they do it in the movies." I could picture it: the big moment when the hero grabs the bank and smashes it against the table. A million dollars in quarters spills out. Urgent soundtrack music pounded in my head.

I rolled the piggy banks over onto their sides. We stared at them, ready for slaughter. This was turning out to be a bit sad.

"What's that?" Bobby Gene pointed at a blue rubber circle on the belly of his pig. Mine had a green one.

"There's a plug!" After a few tugs, it popped right out. Coins poured into my hand.

"Sweet! We don't have to kill them." Bobby Gene opened his own bank.

We shook the coins out and tugged out the bills with hooked fingers. We kept our piles separated with an oversized pencil.

Bobby Gene's bank was quite a bit fuller than mine. I wasn't so happy about that. We'd gotten them at the same time, after all. A Christmas gift from Granddad some years back.

We stacked up our dollar bills and separated the coins by type. That was the easiest way to count, Bobby Gene said.

My total was $27.20. Bobby Gene had a whopping $77.46.

So, had he been keeping more of the change for errands we'd been running together? That wasn't fair. I'd have to keep my eye on him.

"Over a hundred dollars, total!" I exclaimed. "That plus the fireworks is a really good start."

Bobby Gene looked skeptical. "We're a long way from four ninety-nine ninety-five. And I don't think we should give Styx any of this money."

"What? Why not? It'll get us to the moped faster."

"We should wait and see what happens. Dad says never put all your cards on the table, right?"

My skin flushed. Why should Dad get to make all the

rules? "We made a deal with Styx. We're going to get the Grasshopper."

"He's supposed to get *us* money, not the other way around."

I shook my head. Proving ourselves to Styx meant showing him all we had to offer.

Bobby Gene was still talking. "Now that we know we can count our savings anytime, we can keep the banks as backup."

"You can keep yours," I snapped. "I'm not letting you screw this up for both of us."

I snatched up my coins and started to stuff them back into my pig, one by one.

*Clink.*

*Plink.*

"It's just practical, right?" he said.

"Practical and STUPID!" I shouted. Bobby Gene looked shocked. I was shocked. And yet my mouth kept moving.

"People like Styx and me, we're going places." To the city. To the horizon. To infinity. "Don't stand in our way."

*Clink.*

*Plink.*

I needed to make a dramatic exit. I scooped up each careful stack of coins and dumped them into my shirt, holding up the hem like a net. I took the wad of bills into my fist, hugged the piggy bank to my chest and charged up the ladder to my bunk.

The coins poured out on my sheets and I kept on stuffing them. *Clink. Plink. Plunk.*

I glared over the railing. Bobby Gene sat in the middle of the carpet, with a real set look on his face. Why did he have to shoot down my dreams?

"You're going to sleep with that thing up there now?"

"Sure am. You can't have any of it."

My fingers shook but I kept on sliding coins into the slot. What was happening? Why did it feel like everything I'd ever hoped for was slipping away? Bobby Gene and I got into stupid fights all the time, but it had never felt exactly like this before.

*Clink. Plink. Plunk.*

"We've known Styx for like a week," Bobby Gene said. "How come you want to trust him with your savings more than you trust me?"

I didn't have an answer for that one. At least, not in words. In my heart, some kind of answer rose up.

Bobby Gene was everything familiar. Everything I already knew. Styx represented what was possible. All the invisible things that eventually might be seen. And to be seen would change everything.

Silence fell between us as my coins dropped into the bank. *Clink. Plink. Plunk.*

It wasn't the greatest thing to try to do mad. It was slow and precise and I felt stupider and more ordinary with every coin I dropped.

Bobby Gene sighed and started refilling his own bank. The sound of him coming back to me settled my racing heart.

# CHAPTER 13

## A HANDFUL OF TROUBLE

Styx Malone was a handful of trouble. That's what Mom said the first time she laid eyes on him.

He strolled in through the yard to pick us up. Mom saw him through the window and followed us over to meet him at the back door.

That day he was wearing a cap pulled on backward and a little to the side, and shades. The same threadbare jeans and a tight gray T-shirt with the sleeves cut out. "Yo, Mrs. Franklin," he said. "What's good?"

Mom levered the screen door open. "You must be Styx."

"In the flesh." He popped up his shades and smiled like a million bucks. "Pleasure to make your acquaintance." His voice took on a real formal tone, but it was hard to tell if he was being serious. "Hey, guys."

"Hey, Styx," we said, edging past her.

Mom arched her brows at us, but she didn't say, "I don't

want you hanging around that boy." It was written on her face, though, a canyon of disapproval folded between her eyes.

We scooted out the door before the words could slip out of her. Still, the message echoed.

"Let's grab that gunnysack," Styx said when we were out of earshot. "It's time for the next step."

We led the way to the fireworks stash.

"How far is it this time?" Bobby Gene asked. "We have to get permission if we're going beyond Washington Street." As if he needed to remind me. Loudly. In front of Styx.

"Other direction," Styx answered. "You got a boundary over there?" He pointed past the woods, away from town, toward the country road and its endless cornfields.

We didn't, really. But we didn't need one. Past the edge of our neighborhood, there was nothing to see except corn for about forty miles.

"What are we gonna find over there?" Bobby Gene hefted the gunnysack up from behind the fallen log where we'd stashed it.

"You'll see." Styx was forever cryptic. A good spy should lean into intrigue, no matter what. Styx peered into the sack in Bobby Gene's arms. "We should save some of these, I reckon."

"What for?"

"Light up a coupla these, you got yourself a party."

"We want the best possible trade, though," Bobby Gene said. "Don't we?"

Styx shrugged. "A big bag of fireworks is a big bag of fireworks, don'tcha think?"

Bobby Gene's expression swirled into a question mark. He usually got that look on his face when I wanted to do a thing that he wasn't so sure about. Now that we were hanging with Styx Malone, that look came around a lot more often.

"The whole point is to get rid of them," I said. "We don't want to get caught with them." I didn't want us to have to admit that Mom would skin our hides into the next century if she found out we'd ever held any fireworks, let alone set them off.

"We're not really allowed to use them," Bobby Gene confessed, betraying the brotherhood.

Styx grinned with half his mouth. "No kidding, B.G. Believe it or not, I picked up on that."

I sure enough noticed the minute Styx started calling Bobby Gene B.G. I waited to see what his nickname for me was gonna be, but he always kept calling me Caleb.

"If all of us only ever did what we were allowed to do, the world would be a pretty boring place," Styx said.

"That's for sure," I agreed.

"The deal was to get rid of them." Bobby Gene's voice

rose. Uh-oh. This was what his face looked like when he was about to dig in his heels.

Styx read it too. "I take your point about the best trade," he said, his voice low and easy. "We can sell them all today, no problem." He grinned that salesman grin and clapped Bobby Gene on the shoulder. "Let's rock and roll."

We followed Styx through the woods till we hit the county road. He led us all the way to an intersection where the paved road met a dirt road that disappeared off into the corn.

"Check this out," he said. At one corner of the intersection sat a rusted old pickup truck with a FOR SALE sign in the window. Beside it, a dusty-looking riding mower, with a matching sign. Beyond the fields of half-grown corn, a farmhouse jutted up against the landscape.

Styx patted the nose of the riding mower. "Thing of beauty, eh?"

Not really, at least as far as I could tell. It was nothing special, a riding mower like some of our neighbors had, except older and broken. I squinted, trying to see the magic I was missing. Maybe Styx just had a thing for green automotive paint.

"Uh," Bobby Gene said, ever the master wordsmith.

Styx laughed. "I'm kidding. It's just a means to an end. You'll see in a minute."

We kept going along another dirt road, until we met a

chain link fence festooned with KEEP OUT signs. On the other side was a small dirt lot full of random objects. Lots of car tires, machine parts, slouching garbage bags, rusted-out car frames, along with plenty of things I couldn't name.

"What is this place?" I asked.

"Kind of a junkyard, I guess you'd call it. Scrap metal and whatnot."

"Is this the place?" Bobby Gene's face was red from exertion. Those fireworks weren't exactly light.

"You think we can sell the fireworks here?"

"I know a guy." Styx hooked his fingers over the edge of the junkyard fence.

Styx always knew a guy. And right ahead of us, on the other side of the fence, we were steps away from knowing a guy too.

"Isn't this trespassing?" Bobby Gene worried aloud.

"Nah," Styx said. "It's a shortcut."

"Feels wrong," Bobby Gene said.

"Sometimes doing wrong feels right, and vice versa," Styx countered. "We're going to see the guy who runs the place. It's no big."

This exchange should have given me pause.

Instead, I said, "Get with the program, B.G.," and he did.

# CHAPTER 14

## TRESPASSING

Climbing a chain-link fence turned out to be not that easy. You had to have skinny feet like Styx and me, or some kinda quick balance. Bobby Gene had neither.

I scrambled up the fence, which bowed and shimmied under my weight. My heart pounded as I used the KEEP OUT sign for leverage. We were spies. Assassins. Ninjas. Executing a lightning attack so stealthy we didn't even need the cover of night.

Boom. I landed on the ground inside the fence, feeling like a genuine outlaw.

When Styx was up and over, at the top of the fence, he reached back for the gunnysack. Bobby Gene pushed it up to him. Then he struggled to lever his stocky self up and over after us.

He managed it, finally, after hefting himself up and sagging back down a few times. He rolled over the bar and skidded down the inside of the chain link, not bothering to look for footholds. He glared at me like I owed him, so I patted his back. "You did good."

We wound through the piles of junk until we reached a small trailer. Styx ran up and knocked on the door. A scruffy guy with a big mustache poked his head out.

"Hey, Robo."

"What's good, brotha?" The guy slapped palms with Styx. They were both long and skinny like noodles. Their hands smacked, then they pulled them apart, real slick.

"His name is Robo?" Bobby Gene whispered to me.

Robo looked past Styx, nodding to us. "Robert," he explained.

Bobby Gene's face lit up. "Hey, me too!"

"Bet they don't call you that either," Robo said.

"No."

"Too formal-sounding, eh?"

Bobby Gene shrugged. We'd never stopped to wonder why we called him what we called him. It had never really mattered until today, when it earned him a cool nickname.

"Mom says it's so people don't confuse me with Dad," Bobby Gene said.

Oh. Huh. That made sense. There were a lot of Robert Gene Franklins in our family. People called Granddad Robert, Dad was Bobby, and then there was Bobby Gene.

Robo motioned to the gunnysack. "This the loot?"

"Yeah," Styx said. "We need cash money, plus some stuff from the yard."

"What'd you have in mind?"

"Depends on your cash offer," Styx said.

"One hundred."

Styx scoffed. "It's worth more than that. You're looking at three hundred dollars' worth of fireworks, easy."

Three hundred! Bobby Gene and I exchanged shocked looks. I started doing math.

"I'll take a closer look," Robo said. "Show me what you want from the yard."

Bobby Gene stood with him as he sifted through our haul.

Styx and I walked through the junkyard. He gathered all manner of items and handed them to me to carry. Mostly car parts, it seemed. When he turned to me with what looked like an entire bumper in his hand, he paused and laughed. My eyes felt huge in my head.

"Your face," he said, clutching his stomach in amusement. "Hang on."

My arms were already too full. Styx shuffled himself toward a different pile, rummaged for a moment and emerged with an ancient-looking Radio Flyer wagon. The classic kind, but with a janky wheel. We had one of these at home that actually rolled.

We piled the car parts in the wagon. I rolled it along,

easing it over the rutted ground. Styx carried the bumper, seeing as it was almost as long as I was tall.

"I think that's everything," he said. "Let's go negotiate."

"There's more than I thought in here," Robo agreed as we walked up. "But they're illegal. That makes them hard to move."

Bobby Gene's expression soured considerably at this development. I don't know what he was upset about. We knew the bag was trouble all along. Most types of fireworks were illegal in Indiana.

"Nah, you can move 'em. People drive to the border for these," Styx told Robo. "Three hundred. Think about it. Sell them piecewise, you'll pull down five hundred easy."

Bobby Gene perked up at that. "Really? Then why don't we do that?" Out of him, it was an honest question, but Robo slid a suspicious glance his way. Then he laughed.

"Hoo boy." Robo chuckled. "I can see it now."

Styx shot Bobby Gene a "hush up" look.

Robo stuck his chin forward, mulling on it. "I can come up to one fifty," he offered. "Plus what's in the wagon."

"Two hundred," Styx said. "Think about it. There's the value of the fireworks and then the value of them being from out of state. We're saving you a tank of gas each way, for sure."

It was like watching a tennis match, or maybe more like badminton in our backyard. *Pong.* Styx hit the birdie.

It floated up in a long, patient arc, sailed over the net and landed in Robo's court. *Pong.* He sent it back.

"I can get there and back on one tank of gas. And there's a lot in that wagon. One fifty cash. Best and final offer."

Styx stayed chill, but underneath it he must've been a little discouraged. It was a heck of a lot of money, but not enough to get the moped.

"Hang on. Let me confer with my gents a moment." Styx pulled us aside. "This is a good deal. We should take it."

"We need more. Even if we threw in all our savings, we'd still be short," I said. Styx's brow ticked. Bobby Gene's eyes shot daggers at me. Probably for mentioning that we had money we hadn't mentioned before. Oops.

Styx stayed smooth. "Don't forget the trade part. Remember the mower I showed you?"

We nodded.

Styx pointed to the wagonload. "We're gonna trade all this junk for it next."

"What are we gonna do with a busted-up riding mower?" Bobby Gene complained. "We want money."

"Or usable stuff," I added. The whole plan was to trade up for better stuff. Bobby Gene was right. Who was ever going to want that old mower?

Styx patted the air with his hands. "Listen, that mower is worth six, maybe seven hundred bucks once we replace the motor. We can do that, no problem."

"We can?" I was skeptical. "Is there a motor in that wagon?"

"Trust me," Styx says. "I got it."

Six or seven hundred bucks sounded better than one hundred fifty, that was for sure.

"We can pay off Cory with his share of this first deal," Styx said. "He doesn't have to know about the mower trade."

Bobby Gene and I exchanged a glance. Did that count as cheating? It might not exactly be cheating Cory, but it wasn't entirely honest.

"That means we're pulling out way ahead here, cash-wise," Styx said.

"I guess," Bobby Gene said. To be honest, one hundred and fifty bucks was more money than we'd ever seen in one place. Couldn't very well pass that up. Especially since priority number one was to get that trouble magnet of a gunnysack off our hands.

"Sure," I said. "Let's tell Robo we have a deal."

# CHAPTER 15

## SLIPPERY

We lugged the janky wagon back toward the crossroads. Styx gazed over the field at the farmhouse. He sighed. "Truck's gone. He's not home. Guess it'll have to wait."

"We should get home anyway," Bobby Gene said. "Mom's gonna start to wonder what we're doing."

We started toward home. "What are you going to tell her we did all afternoon?" Styx asked.

"Hung with you in the woods," I said.

At the same time as Bobby Gene said, "Went to the playground."

Styx laughed. "You two best get your stories straight."

"It was all afternoon," I argued. "We could've done both."

"Fair enough." He tapped the side of his head. "But you don't wanna go in there improvising. Always get your cover story straight."

That was good advice. It brought me back to my spy training. If we were going to play by our own rules, we'd have to bone up on our acting skills. Neither one of us had a quick-thinking way with words like Styx did.

"Hey, Styx, did you ever pull off an escalator trade before?" Bobby Gene asked.

"Absolutely." Styx grinned. "Lots of times." He paused, listened to our eager silence for a moment. "Why? You want to hear about that?"

"Yeah!" we exclaimed.

Styx rolled out his tales real slow, keeping us on the hook. "This one time, I traded an old microwave till I got a grill for the backyard." He thumbed over his shoulder, as if we could see all the way to his house from here.

"Another time, I traded a harmonica till I got this here iPod." He pulled the tiny device out of his pocket.

"Where'd you get the harmonica?" Bobby Gene asked.

"Found it. All rusted out and nasty." Styx shook his head. "One man's junk makes another man's fortune. It's amazing what you can do with a little rust remover and some elbow grease."

We stared at the flat silver rectangle in his palm. Proof positive that the escalator trade was possible. Styx bounced it gently and caught it in his fist, then tucked it away. "Talk about getting something for nothing."

Styx pulled the wad of cash from his pocket. He counted

out fifty dollars and handed it to me. "This is Cormier's cut. You can give it to him tomorrow."

I took the money.

"As for the rest," Styx suggested, "why don't we stash the wagon at your place, and I'll hang on to the cash."

I was holding fifty bucks in my hand right then, so I would've agreed to anything Styx Malone suggested.

Bobby Gene did not feel the same. "How about we split the cash like we said we would?"

A slow smile spread across Styx's face. "Equal risk, equal rewards." He shuffled through the stack of bills and handed Bobby Gene our portion. "I really like how you guys operate."

"So, we trade the parts for the mower, fix the mower, and then trade the mower for the moped?" I asked.

"Basically," Styx said.

"Four ninety-nine ninety-five, plus tax," Bobby Gene whispered. I could hear the question in his voice. Would the escalator trade really work?

Styx grinned and fanned the cash. "Plus tax, and then some. We'll have enough left over for a couple fried chicken dinners."

"Extra biscuits," Bobby Gene chimed in, his voice dreamy. My stomach growled.

The sky was still full of late-afternoon light. It must be getting close to dinnertime. For shizzle, as Styx would say.

"A heck of a celebration, for sure," Styx assured us. "When it's all said and done, and we've had our first rides."

"How long's it going to take?" I asked.

Styx looked at the sky. "I don't know," he said. "I guess we'll have to wait and see."

I had more questions for Styx. A hundred more. A thousand more. All the questions that the world might answer between the time a person is ten and the time he becomes sixteen. With a driver's license and the power to negotiate 150 cash dollars out of someone else's pocket.

But right then, Mom's voice reached us, all the way out here in the trees. "Bobby Gene! Caleb! Dinner!"

"That's my cue to fade into the shadows," Styx said. "You boys have a good night."

"Night, Styx," we said.

"Catch you later." He tilted his cap toward his ear, then sauntered away through the yard. His feet shushed against the grass. I tried to absorb him, to copy his way of moving, of being. But it wasn't that easy.

Mom was wrong about Styx being a handful of trouble. He wasn't a handful of anything. He was a pile of sand, slipping through our fingers.

# CHAPTER 16

## PROFITS AND PAYOFFS

We rode into Cory Cormier's yard at half past ten the next morning. Cory was sitting on the porch steps with a shovel in his hand, waiting for us.

"You're late."

"I guess." We dropped our bikes on the grass. "But you'll be happy with why, today."

"Why?" Cory made a move as if to cross his arms, annoyed-like. But he was holding the shovel in one hand so it didn't quite work.

I held back my snicker, just barely.

"Let's go around back," Bobby Gene suggested. The front of Cory's house was all windows. Nothing said "Mom's watching" like seven giant panes of glass. Especially when the sun glare made it much too bright to see in from the outside.

"What's the shovel for?"

"We have to turn the compost," Cory informed us. "And that won't take an hour, so then she's got us washing the outside windows."

"That's way more than an hour," I complained. Cory's house was not large, but it was built up on a high brick foundation. To reach the windows, we'd have to use a ladder and everything. "What gives with that?"

"We can finish tomorrow, she said."

"We have to remember to keep an eye on the time, though," Bobby Gene reminded us. "And not get distracted."

He was right. When Cory's mom had had us wash both family cars, we'd lost track of time and finished the whole job. Three hours, that cost us. There *might* have been an elaborate sponge fight that took up a chunk of those hours, but still.

There was only one shovel, so we took turns at the compost pile. Three scoops each, and then hand off the shovel. That made it slow, but fair. It wasn't as smelly as you'd expect a bunch of rotting food to be. The occasional peach pit or banana peel surfaced as we scooped.

"Good news," I reported as I handed off the shovel to Cory.

"We sold the apple cart," Bobby Gene said.

"The fireworks? Great."

Cory was clearly not cut out for stealth work.

"The whole point of a code word is that you don't have

to say the real thing," I reminded him. I pointed at the house. "Especially where certain people might hear you?"

"Oh, right." Cory winked dramatically. "The *apple cart*." Sheesh.

"Anyway, here's your cut." Bobby Gene pulled the roll of bills from his pocket and forked them over.

Cory's eyes bugged. "Whoa."

Those fifty bucks sure looked fat and happy sitting in Cory's palm. Bobby Gene'd had the bright idea to swap out a couple of Robo's twenties with some of our piggy bank singles. This had a double benefit: more space for our savings, plus it made the offering to Cory look absolutely huge.

"Yeah, Styx got us more than we expected," Bobby Gene said.

Cory's face darkened at the mention of Styx. He glanced over our shoulders. "He's not coming here, right?"

"We don't need him to mediate anymore, do we?" I said. "The deal is done."

Cory pocketed the cash by way of agreement.

✦ ✦ ✦

"How'd it go?" Styx asked when we met that afternoon.

"We're in the clear," I said. "Cory's happy."

"Let's check on the stash," Styx said. "Has your dad got any tools?"

We showed him the shed. He selected a few simple items. A regular wrench, a socket wrench, pliers.

We emptied the wagon and flipped it over. Styx took the wrenches and went to work on the broken wheel.

"It looks pretty messed up," Bobby Gene said. His voice oozed skepticism.

"Anything's fixable," Styx said. He pried at the bent axle till it groaned.

"Anything?" I didn't really mean to say it out loud.

"Anything with metal parts, I mean." Styx kept working. Didn't raise his head. "Why? What do you want to fix so bad?"

The woods fell still. No breeze. I thought about BREAKING NEWS, ordinary things, our empty seats on the bus to the museum.

"Seems like you got it pretty good," Styx added.

"I don't want to be ordinary." It wasn't the right words. At least, it wasn't all of them.

Bobby Gene sighed like the world was ending. "Here we go again."

Styx glanced up then. "You feeling dissatisfied?"

Dissatisfied.

"Yeah," I said. "Dissatisfied." The word tasted like the feeling. Like a mouthful of vinegar or the sound of never-ending bad news.

"That's good. You know why?"

I didn't.

"Dissatisfaction is the first step on the road to greatness." Styx pointed the socket wrench at me. "You wanna make a change?"

"Yeah."

"All the way to the bottom of your heart and back?"

I put my whole self into answering. "Yeah."

Our eyes locked. Styx's power arced into me. "Then nobody can stop you."

Styx righted the wagon. He rocked it side to side, testing its stability. "People who like things exactly the same aren't the ones who go out and change the world."

"We're world-changers?" It felt like he had pinned a badge to my chest. One made of gold dust and sunshine.

Styx handed me the wagon handle. "Only if you want to be."

I tugged. Sure enough, it rolled straight. Impressive.

"So can we take it to the other guy now?"

"We'll try on Saturday," Styx said. "It's the best time to catch him." He plucked a rusty metal box off the pile of goods and set it aside. "Except this. We'll need this later."

"What is it?" I asked. The box had some kind of images on the side. They were too covered in dirt and rust to be recognizable.

"We'll find out when we clean it up," Styx said. "I know

a guy who likes this sort of thing, and it might be worth something to us, is all."

"Where'd you learn to fix stuff?" Bobby Gene asked as we reloaded the wagon.

"Yeah, and can you teach us?" I added.

Styx raised a shoulder. "Guess I picked it up somewhere." That quick shrug was becoming very familiar. It was like a little shimmy, his way of sliding out from under an answer. Maybe he could only forget the truth with one shoulder at a time.

But we didn't know that much about Styx yet. It didn't occur to us to study his every move or to wonder what he was hiding. How could he have been hiding anything? He was too busy showing us a whole new world.

# CHAPTER 17

## THE LIMITLESS MAGIC OF STYX MALONE

The first time Styx came for dinner, well, it started out as a disaster. He knew his manners perfectly well, he just didn't like to use them. He rubbed his mouth with his hands, then wiped them on his jeans. Things like that.

Mom watched him, quiet. Her lips pursed, like they were stuck in a pre-scold, but she held it back. Styx had that effect.

Right when it seemed like she was about to say something against him, he'd smile. "This rice is delicious, Mrs. Franklin," he'd say. Mom had made her style rice, soaked in buttery mushroom sauce.

Mom ruffled her napkin. "I'm glad you like it."

Styx knew how to find the line. Dance right on top of it. Tip his hat. I admired that.

"What grade are you in, Styx?"

"Round about tenth," he said, his mouth full of salad. I'll say this for Styx—he cleaned his plate, no complaints.

"Round about? Does that mean going in or coming out?"

Styx shrugged. "What's the difference? It's just school."

"What do you plan to do when you graduate?"

Geez. Mom was grilling Styx just as good as the fish.

Styx tipped a shoulder and shoveled in more lettuce. "Get a job. Rule the world."

His leafy grin caused Bobby Gene to snort-cough into his juice.

"What sort of job interests you?" Mom's voice was syrupy. That meant she was closing in for the kill.

"Styx has been to the Children's Museum ten times," I reported, hoping to get him off the hot seat. "He likes the science exhibits best."

"That's nice," Dad said. His attention was on the style rice. He laid a few grains on Susie's tray, then dug back in.

"I'm fixing to check it out again one of these days," Styx said.

"Maybe we could all go together," I suggested, glancing sideways at Dad.

Dad shook his head slowly. "No cause to go into the city."

Which is what he always said, so I don't know why in this case it started me simmering. "You never let us go anywhere," I complained. We were less than thirty minutes from the edge of the city, and barely forty-five from the heart of things. Even when there was traffic.

"Caleb." Mom did the thing where she only said one word but put a lot of tone into it.

Dad set down his fork. "This discussion is over."

"No." I tried to hold myself back, but I couldn't. My voice had tone now too. The tone of whine.

"We're small-town folk, Caleb. Everything we need is right here." Dad reached over and squeezed Mom's hand.

I dropped my face into my hands, horrified. Dad was making us sound like country bumpkins.

"It's better that way," he said.

I didn't understand. Dad grew up in Indy. He knew the city through and through—all the lights, the buildings, the sights and the people—yet for some reason he preferred the middle of nowhere.

"Better for who?" I couldn't stop myself. Bobby Gene sighed, no doubt anticipating the lecture that was coming. *We're safe here. People know us here.*

"Caleb—"

My heart stung. All the way down to the bottom and back. My fingers curled around the edge of the table. My lungs were working overtime.

I wanted a change. No one could stop me.

"Dad—"

"You're right, Mr. Franklin." Styx spoke over me, his voice as smooth as Mom's butter sauce. "This is a great town." He smiled at Dad. "You a Pacers fan? Colts? You ever ball?"

"Oh, yeah," Dad said. "Defensive back, Fourth Ridge High."

"I know Fourth Ridge." Styx nodded. "Good team."

"Back in the day, yeah. They've gone downhill."

"Shame," Styx commiserated.

My fingers slowly relaxed. Styx winked at me, then shook his head. Not now, it seemed he was saying.

Dad nodded. "Sat on the bench at IU. Got on the field twice, though. Against Iowa, against Notre Dame." He looked at the centerpiece, a wooden vase of what he called "durable flowers." His gaze turned distant for a moment, then he grinned. "Good times."

"You played Big Ten? That's serious bragging rights," Styx acknowledged.

Dad grinned again. "That's how I wooed Angie here. She was a sucker for my sweet moves on the field."

"And off, I bet," Styx said.

"Ew," Bobby Gene and I chorused.

Even Mom cracked a smile at that one. Styx Malone, miracle worker.

"You play ball?" Dad asked.

Styx raised a shoulder. "I can hold my own in the schoolyard."

Dad looked pleased. "Hey, we should all toss it around one evening." It was like pulling teeth to get me and Bobby Gene to play ball. I didn't have interest; Bobby Gene couldn't hit the broad side of a barn, as they say. But he was built like a linebacker, which didn't involve ball skills at all, so Dad held out hope.

"That sounds great, Mr. Franklin," Styx said. "We'll do that."

"But not tonight," Mom said. "It's getting dark, and it's time for dessert. Bobby Gene?"

Luckily he was the one who got tagged to help clear. I could barely sit still. Styx loved the museum *and* could fix everything *and* he knew how to talk to Dad?

The feeling at the bottom of my heart was still there. Dissatis⁁ied. But maybe I had more to learn from Styx before I could properly fight my battle.

We enjoyed strawberry shortcake for dessert, and then it was time for Styx to go.

"I'll drive you home," Dad said. "No cause to be roaming around after dark."

"Nah, it's just over the woods," Styx said. Dad hesitated.

"Not a house between here and there," Styx added. "I'm okay."

Dad frowned. "Well, I'll walk you out." He stalked to the back porch like someone was forcing him.

"Thanks for being cool about things," I whispered as we walked Styx to the door. "Sorry we can't go to the museum together."

"Don't sweat it, Caleb, my man." He gave my thoughts a

little nudge with his eyebrows. "Where there's a will there's a way, you know what I'm saying?"

I did. Styx's secret message cut through my frustration like a knife. The Grasshopper was the key. When it was ours, we could go anywhere. We could ride all the way into Indy. We could chill at the museum. Styx could show us everything, and Dad would never need to know.

At the door, Styx turned around. He slapped our hands in the way he'd shown us. Slap, curl fingers together, slap and slide away easy. He could do it with both of us at the same time, one on each hand. Real smooth. He tugged up his jeans to almost cover his boxers. Smiled over at Mom, standing behind us. Gave a little bow.

"Thank you, ma'am. That was a right good supper." Styx had sure eaten enough of it too. No leftover style rice for us this time.

"You're welcome in our house anytime," Mom said.

Behind her back, Bobby Gene made a "huh" face, and I can't say I blamed him. Mom was full of surprises tonight.

Styx smiled, the usual knowing way. "I'm more of an outdoor cat," he said.

"Very well. Boys, tell Styx good night."

"See you tomorrow," we said, waving.

Bobby Gene and I started clearing the dessert plates. We scraped everything and loaded the dishwasher. Then we held out our fists.

Bobby Gene counted it off. "One, two, three, shoot."

"Ha." My rock crushed his scissors, so he scrubbed the pots and I dried.

We dried our hands, only to find Mom lingering behind us, bouncing Susie to sleep. Her expression said a bit of damage control was in order.

"That was a great dinner," I told her. "Styx was really impressed."

"This is your new friend?" Mom said. The war in her eyes clashed right over my head. She wanted to trust us. Trust was a thing with Mom. That and giving people the benefit of the doubt. But Styx was a lot to take.

# CHAPTER 18

## PIXIE

"We're going to walk to the pond," I told Mom. I figured it was best not to mention that we'd be inviting Styx to come along.

"Fishing?" Mom asked, wearing half a smile. We liked to go fishing, but we never came home with any fish.

"Yep."

We scampered through the woods lugging our three poles and the ever-important catch bucket. The path to Styx's place was familiar now. Although we had never actually been all the way to Styx's house. He generally met us at the usual tree, a.k.a. his office.

Today we skipped right past the copse of birch trees and into the clearing. Unlike on our side of the woods, it didn't open up into a whole neighborhood full of houses. There was just one house, carved into a small break in the trees. A long dirt driveway snaked away toward the nearest road.

Styx's house was mostly brown, a mix of fake-wood siding and peeling paint. The area around the house felt more hushed even than the woods, which was strange.

We paused in the yard. Maybe, if we lingered here, he would appear.

The house had a huge wood-planked back porch that looked more like a front porch, the way it stretched all along the width of the house and was kind of narrow. It took four steps to get up to it. And it was covered, with thin sheets of something that looked like plywood. Painted brown, of course. Held up by a series of metal pipes as thin as dowel rods.

All in all, the porch had the effect of a cool-looking clubhouse. It made the house seem less real, or something. Not quite a place where anyone would actually live.

Bobby Gene glanced at me, uncertain. "So, should we knock?"

Styx was our friend. Our business partner, too. Why did it feel like we were trespassing?

"Yeah, I guess."

The door was open, with the screen closed and latched to keep bugs out. A knock on the screen-door frame had a hollow sound. Not nearly as definitive as knuckles on wood.

We waited.

Through the screen, we could see a hallway leading toward a kitchen. An up staircase occupied part of the view.

"Maybe he's not home," Bobby Gene suggested.

I didn't like the thought of Styx somewhere else in the world, exploring without us. I clapped my fist against the screen door a second time.

A girl floated into view. She was small, blond, and frowning. "Please continue to wait," she said. "I'm not dressed for company."

She flitted away, like some kind of wood sprite. She wore jean shorts and a thin white tank top. And a long garland of flowers, draped over her elbows like a feather boa. Petals trailed behind her up the stairs.

Bobby Gene stared after her. "That was . . . strange."

*Strange* didn't begin to cover it.

"Maybe this isn't his house," Bobby Gene said. "We don't really know for sure."

But it had to be his house. This was where Styx always came from, so this was where he must be.

Sure enough, the next thing we saw was Styx Malone himself. He bounded down the stairs, thumping with each step. Unlike the girl, who hadn't made a sound.

"Oh, hey, guys." He popped out and joined us on the porch.

"Hey, Styx."

He smiled then, in a way that made him look younger. "I wasn't sure, after last night, with your dad—"

"We're going fishing. Want to come?" I cut him off. The

space between Styx and us was supposed to be different than home. With Styx we were free in every possible way.

Styx furrowed his brow and pulled in his lip. "Huh. Never been fishing."

"It's easy," we assured him.

"Yeah, sure," he agreed. "I can do that."

We strolled off the porch and into the yard. We had almost made it to the tree line when the screen creaked behind us.

The blond girl darted onto the porch. "Wait for me," she called.

She was still wearing the jean shorts, but no longer carrying the floral boa. She now wore a feathery tank top splashed with all kinds of colors. Around her waist bloomed one of those starchy pink ballerina skirts. Dressing for company meant impersonating a crazy flower, apparently.

"Who's that?" Bobby Gene said.

Styx turned. "That's my sister."

"What?" Bobby Gene blurted. Probably on account of the fact that Styx was dark as night and she was lighter than milk. Bobby and Susie and I were pretty much the same sort of middle brown.

"Sis-ter," Styx repeated, drawing it out like Bobby Gene was slow. "You know, the girl with the room next to mine? Causes me pains in my butt?"

"Oh," Bobby Gene said. "Sure."

She twirled her way closer. The sequins on her tutu

caught the light and glinted like jewels. She spun dizzily to a stop in front of us. "I'm Pixie," she chirped. "Who are you?"

Bobby Gene snickered.

Styx fixed him with a long, sharp, pinning stare. "Sister" was all he said. And from that moment on, neither of us ever said another word against her. It would be a while before we learned how deep it went, but once Styx found a thing to like about you, he had your back for life.

"Caleb. Bobby Gene," I said, pointing to us in turn.

Pixie wore a zebra-striped headband with black-and-pink mouse ears poking up off it. She was my age, I guess, though all the twirling made her seem more like a little kid.

"Her name is Penny," Styx informed us.

"Call me Pixie," she insisted.

"Are you going to tell them why?" Styx said wryly.

Pixie crossed her arms. "It's personal."

Styx had this little smile on his face now. It was funny. He seemed like a different kind of guy with her around. Softer, but no less cool.

I didn't really care what her name was—the thing that seemed worth explaining to me was the mouse ears.

"We're going fishing," I informed her. Dealing in facts seemed wise at this juncture.

"Fishing is cruel." The words floated up out of the whirlwind that was Pixie.

Bobby Gene chimed in. "Not the way we do it."

I laughed. Styx cocked his head, curious.

Pixie paused her twirling and regarded us more seriously. "I can see why Styx finds you interesting," she said.

"Penny!" A woman's voice echoed from within the silent house. "Get a move on, Miss Thing."

Pixie spun straight into my personal space. "I can't go fishing," she said. "I have a prior appointment. Invite me again sometime?"

I wasn't a hundred percent sure we'd invited her this time. "Uh, yeah. Cool," I said.

The screen door creaked and the woman emerged. From this distance, she was barely more than a silhouette in the shadows of the porch. She appeared compact and plump at the same time. Like a snowman on stilts. When she poked her head into the light, she had long, light hair, much more similar to Pixie than Styx.

Pixie spiraled away from us, glinting and glittering. The girl really knew how to make a showstopping entrance and exit. There was something to that, I supposed.

"How'd you end up with a sister?" Bobby Gene asked.

"You live long enough, you pick up a few things," Styx said, raising a shoulder.

# CHAPTER 19

## GONE . . . FISHING?

Bobby Gene handed Styx the third fishing pole and we traipsed into the woods. They kept on talking, the two of them, but my mind drifted. I was thinking about things, like how to make an entrance, and the line between *special* and *weird*.

"I didn't know there was a pond," Styx was saying. "And I thought I'd explored the woods pretty well."

"It's not even that far," Bobby Gene assured him. "But you have to walk the exact right way, or else you'll never find it."

Our pond was nestled in an unusually dense section of woods. The land surrounding it was rockier than any other place we knew, and the path to it branched off underneath a massive fallen oak that looked somewhat like a mermaid. If you squinted.

It was strange approaching it from the other side. We

had to keep turning around to look for our usual landmarks, but eventually we found the mermaid tree.

"There she is." Bobby Gene sounded relieved. We ducked under, and the path continued. Styx seemed impressed with our navigational know-how. Flora and fauna. Covered.

The woods thickened briefly, then the leaves opened up and the sky returned in all its midsummer glory. The pond was large, and deep enough to swim in, although we weren't allowed to swim alone here. Last summer we tried to argue that we weren't alone because we were together. That got no traction with Mom.

Our favorite spot was at the mouth of the brook that trickled over the rocks and into the pond. It was a very small waterfall, but it was ours. We liked to sit on the log that jutted out across the brook and let our legs dangle into the water.

"Here," we told Styx. We laid down the fishing poles and climbed up onto the log. Bobby Gene went first, which put me in the middle and Styx on the end. That was how I wanted it. Our legs went down far enough to touch the brook water. Styx's went all the way down to touch the top of the pond. He braced his hands against the log as if to push himself off into the water.

"Looks good enough to swim in," he mused.

"We don't usually swim," I blurted out, before Bobby Gene could say we weren't allowed.

Styx nodded. "And we didn't bring towels or anything. Next time."

"Next time," I heard myself saying. Bobby Gene cut a glance at me, but he didn't speak. Maybe he was imagining how good it would feel to pop off our shirts and shorts and take a quick dip. Maybe we couldn't consider ourselves "alone" since Styx was with us.

"So what do you guys do when you come here?"

"Talk about stuff," Bobby Gene said. We liked the sound of the water, and the look of the rocks. The feel of the breeze. It was like being in a different place. Not home, but not away, either.

"Who would win in a fight?" I suggested. "Wolverine or Batman?"

"Wolverine," Styx said, at the same time as Bobby Gene said, "Batman."

"Wolverine is wild. Invincible. Victory is in his bones, literally," Styx insisted. This was the position I always took. Secretly, I was glad Styx agreed.

Bobby Gene countered. "Batman has gadgets for everything, and an unlimited budget."

That familiar debate alone chewed up a good ten minutes. Then we took turns suggesting and voting.

"Luke Skywalker or Princess Leia," Bobby Gene said.

"Luke from which movie, and Leia from which movie?" Styx asked. "You gotta be specific."

Oh, I liked that. Styx was making this game more fun. We got a whole debate out of which Luke and which Leia were most powerful.

"Underdog or Rocky the Flying Squirrel?" Styx suggested.

"Who?" we asked.

Styx shook his head. "Too vintage. Never mind. How about Wonder Woman or Mystique?"

"Mystique's a shapeshifter, so she always wins," I said. "She can look like anyone."

"Fair point. But what if she's against another shapeshifter? Like Amethyst from *Steven Universe*?"

Whoa. That was a good one too.

Styx was on a roll. "Princess Leia with a lightsaber versus Princess Leia with a blaster."

"That's a good one," I mused. "Lightsabers are stronger, but Leia is more skilled with a blaster."

"Wait, what? You can't make it a person against themself," Bobby Gene protested.

"Why not?" Styx argued. "It's all made up."

Bobby Gene was confused. "Nobody fights themself."

"Everybody fights themself," Styx answered. "It's the human condition."

"But shapeshifters don't have to," I suggested. "Because they can just change whenever they want." If only it was that easy for the rest of us.

"Here we go," Styx said. "Mystique, shapeshifted to look like Leia with a lightsaber, versus Amethyst, shapeshifted to look like Leia with a blaster."

We stared at him. This was beyond next-level. He'd just upped our game like a boss.

Bobby Gene frowned. "You're messing up the game," he said. "It's supposed to be easy."

The water in the brook gurgled and the frogs splashed. Squirrels darted in the trees, stirring the leaves. Birdsong echoed. All the sounds of summer.

But nothing was the same. My mind spun around everything Styx's questions stirred up. Bobby Gene was wrong. It wasn't too complicated. It was genius.

# CHAPTER 20

## HAPPY ENDINGS

On Saturday, we walked back to the farmhouse, lugging the fixed wagon and all the truck parts. The busted-up riding mower and the rusted-out pickup still stood waiting, right there at the corner of cornfield and cornfield.

Bobby Gene eyed the mower. "Are you sure that thing is fixable?"

"I checked it out," Styx said. "Nothing wrong with it except it's got a busted motor."

We left the wagon there, since no one was likely to come by in the time it took us to make our deal. We crossed the field and knocked on the guy's door.

First we heard barking. Then pawing and whimpering.

Through the wood: "Down, girl."

Finally, the door opened up.

He was a thin man, with a ruddy, square face. He had a

brightness behind his eyes that struck me as unusual. His outfit was very usual—roughed-up overalls of denim so faded it was almost white, and sturdy outdoor boots.

"Oh, it's you," he said. He worked his jaw like he wished he had some chaw going.

"Yeah," Styx said. "Told you I'd be back. These are my associates." He indicated us.

"Pleased to meet you, sir," we said.

The farmer regarded us with his bright gaze. "You're Bobby Franklin's boys, ain't you?"

"That's right," Bobby Gene said.

It was impossible to go anywhere in this town. I racked my brain trying to think if we knew him. The mailbox at the end of the drive had said MADDOX.

"Mr. Maddox, we've got a great deal for you," I told him, pulling myself tall.

"Well, all right," the farmer said. He crossed his arms. "Let's hear it."

"We could tell you, or we could show you," Styx said. "Want to come out and take a look at what we brought?"

Mr. Maddox worked his jaw. "You got a problem with dogs?"

Truth be told, we had a bit of a problem. We'd never had one of our own, so we didn't quite know what to do around them. This was one of the biggest dogs I'd ever seen.

"Nah," Styx said. "She's cute."

Mr. Maddox swished his finger, and the large dog rushed through the door. She began circling our legs and barking in earnest. She sniffed and nudged and rubbed against us.

"Whoa, Bunny. Take it easy, there." The farmer snapped his fingers and the dog returned to his side.

*Bunny?* Bobby Gene and I exchanged wide-eyed glances.

"Uh, what kind is she?" I asked. I thought that was the right question.

"English mastiff," he answered. "She's a sweet dog, just gets excited when there are people."

Mr. Maddox and Bunny the giant mastiff accompanied us back across the field. The dog was very well-behaved, but energetic and curious all the while.

Styx showed Mr. Maddox the wagon. "This is everything you need to fix the truck. You'll get a better price for it now."

Bunny circled the mower, sniffing for the perfect place to do her own business. She squatted happily beside the mower's tire. Bobby Gene stared at the massive pile she left behind.

I returned my attention to the deal in motion. "We'll trade all the truck parts to you in exchange for the mower," I said. "That's a good deal."

Mr. Maddox considered it. "I reckon. But what are you kids gonna do with a broken-down mower?"

"That's our business," Styx said.

"You're not gonna be able to move it from this spot until it's drivable," Mr. Maddox warned.

"You okay with that?" Styx asked. "It's gonna take us some time, but we'll get it done."

"It's gonna sit here one way or the other," Mr. Maddox acknowledged. "No skin off my nose."

"So that's a deal, then?" Styx confirmed.

Mr. Maddox nodded. "Sure thing. Saves me a couple of headaches." He reached out and shook Styx's hand.

I stepped up so that he'd shake mine too. "Thanks kindly, Mr. Maddox."

He worked his jaw. "Just business," he said. "Y'all take care." He snapped his fingers and Bunny dutifully followed him as he headed home across the field.

"Cool beans," Bobby Gene said. "So I guess we own this now?"

Styx plucked the FOR SALE sign off the mower seat and tossed it into the bed of the pickup. "Yup. It's ours."

It was the biggest object we had ever laid claim to. Bobby Gene and I stood reverently before the mower's front grille. Styx was doing something similar around back.

"Ready to go?" Bobby Gene asked.

"Hang on a sec." Styx stood with his hands on the back of the mower.

Bobby Gene raised his eyebrow. "Are you praying or something?"

It did kinda look like maybe he was blessing the thing.

Styx closed his eyes. "I just want to feel the moment, you know?"

I sure liked the sound of that.

"When things go my way, I like to stop time. Just for a second."

"Why?" I asked. When Styx talked like this, I had to know more.

"Shh," he said.

I licked my lips, tried to swallow. Then closed my eyes. To feel the moment.

The moment felt like Saturday, like summer heat, like adventure. It felt as big as the sky above us and as firm as the ground beneath. It felt like the soft swish of corn tassels and being one step closer to an impossible dream.

"Can you feel it?" he whispered.

"Oh, yeah."

Styx blew out a breath. He lightly smacked the mower, the way you might pat a horse on the rump. "One step closer to our happy ending."

He rounded the mower toward us . . . and stepped right in the doggy doo.

"Perfect," he muttered.

"Oh, *gross,*" Bobby Gene said.

I cringed. "No happy ending off that one."

Styx moonwalked through a patch of grass, like it was no biggie. "A happy ending depends on where you stop the story."

Whoa. That was deep.

"What?" Bobby Gene's voice rose like a bubble in water. Bobby Gene does not do deep. "A story is a story. It begins and then it ends."

"You sure?" Styx grinned. "What happened before the beginning? What happened after the end?"

"Nothing," Bobby Gene said. "That's not part of the story."

"Say you're reading a comic," Styx said. "When you finish it, the hero usually wins. But if you kept reading five pages into the next issue and stopped . . ."

Bobby Gene's face reddened. "But that's not the end. Everything's fine in the end."

"If you stop the story there, it's the end," I said. "I get that."

Bobby Gene stewed. We walked.

We were still high on the victory in hand. The road seemed shorter, the world a bit brighter.

Styx reached into his pocket for his candy cigarette pack. He offered us two, but we declined. It was Styx's thing, really. One of many things I wanted to understand but didn't.

He pretended to light it and puff on it. I watched him out the corner of my eye. Wondering.

Wondering, but not having the words. There was always another layer.

We walked in silence this way for a while.

The thought that had been circling in my mind like a vulture finally settled. "Hey, Styx," I said. "Did you ever have a happy ending?"

Styx cut his gaze toward me. He puffed the candy cigarette, then eased it down to his side. "Nah," he said. "Not that I know of."

# CHAPTER 21

## LIMO

We picked Styx up at his office. The plan was to go check on the Grasshopper. We also needed some supplies, so we'd brought along twenty dollars from the fireworks trade. The next phase—acquiring the motor—would be a bit more complicated, Styx had told us. It would take us a few days to get ready.

We strolled up to his office.

"Hey, Styx," we said.

"Hey."

"Hey." Another voice floated down at us from on high.

We looked up. "Hey, Pixie."

She hung upside down, with her knees hooked over a branch about twelve feet up. Her cheeks drooped toward her eyes and her hair pointed straight toward the ground, making her look like a dangling troll doll. The mouse-ear headband contributed to the effect considerably.

"Come on up," she said. "The leaves are very refreshing."

"You are nutty," I answered.

Pixie nodded. "I'm mostly pecans. With just a soupçon of maple sugar."

Styx and I laughed out loud.

"They make coupons for being weird?" Bobby Gene asked. "That figures."

"Soupçon," Pixie repeated. "It means a tiny dab. But . . . more fancy-like."

"We're going downtown," I told her.

"No, thank you," she said. "I'm communing."

So we left her dangling like a psychedelic squirrel and headed for town. All thoughts drifted toward Mission: Grasshopper. We were stealth agents on reconnaissance.

"You think it's gonna get sold before we're ready?" I asked. My stomach tightened at the thought. What if it was all for nothing?

Styx puffed on a candy cigarette. "Nah. But it makes good sense to check on it now and again. When the time comes, there'll be less hassle if we know all the salespeople and the owner. By the time we're done, he'll be begging to give us the thing."

Styx didn't seem worried about anything. He assumed it would all line up exactly the way we wanted. As he led the way through the woods, I swear, the breeze blew just right to open the path for him. He never had to duck or push aside a stray branch. I wondered what it felt like to move through the world like that.

"Plus, we need the rust remover." Styx glanced at us. "You brought cash?"

"Yeah. What's it for?" Bobby Gene asked.

"We gotta clean up that old lunch box so we can trade it for a motor."

My face wrinkled of its own accord. "Who's gonna want that old thing?"

Styx grinned. "Relax. I got this."

We took our usual route downtown, and ran into a bit of a crowd. The street in front of Dickson & Morris was lined with parked cars.

"Funeral today," Bobby Gene said. We didn't think anything of it. Sutton was full of old people. In the mornings Dad handed us the comics out of the paper and flipped over to the obituaries just to make sure everyone we knew was still alive and kicking. This very morning, it had gone something like this:

"Biddy Cunningham. That sounds familiar. Babe?"

Mom shook her head. We didn't know her.

"Huh. Eighty-six. Died in her sleep. That's a good long life."

The sound of Dad's papers rustling, over the crunch of our Honey Nut Cheerios.

"Bill Randall?"

Mom shook her head.

*Rustle. Crunch.*

Bobby Gene slurped his milk and Mom slid him the side-eye.

*Rustle. Crunch. Slurp.*

Dad sighed. "The Cubs, man. Can't catch a break this season." And that was the end of that.

We strolled on by the funeral home, like we'd done a thousand times before, but today one unusual thing did happen. We happened to be going by at the moment a fancy limo arrived. Not the one for the body. That one was already parked right by the curb.

The limo was not the normal black. It was gunmetal gray, and glinting in the sunlight. A uniformed driver slid out from behind the wheel. He came around and opened the back door, then stood beside it, waiting. We scampered past, trying to look at the limo but also stay out of the way. Out of respect and stuff.

"Whoa, check out that limo," I whispered.

"Totally."

"So shiny."

"There's probably a TV inside and everything."

"For sure." Bobby Gene and I riffed about it all the way down the block.

We'd ridden in a limo when Grandma Noonie died. We were supposed to be all sad, and we were, but it was also fun to bounce on the seats. And zip the windows up and down. And open and close the minibar while saying things like "Jeeves, I'd like another." "At your service, sir."

Mom had cried. Dad had yelled. We'd giggled into our lapels, and we laughed out loud now, remembering.

Styx was quiet. The candy cigarette balanced on the edge of his lip. His gaze, half vacant, was directed at the long car too.

The driver nodded sedately to us as we passed.

"Hey, Styx, you ever ride in a limo?"

We waited. Any moment now, Styx would launch into some outlandish tale that could not possibly be true, unless he was some kind of celebrity. *This one time . . .*

We made it all the way to the corner before he answered us.

"Once," he said.

# CHAPTER 22

## FATHERS AND SONS

Styx stayed quiet the rest of the way to the hardware store.

The salesman fussed over us the second we walked in. "You're back. Good timing. Mr. Davis is here." He pointed us toward aisle six. Standing there was a lean and leathery man holding a clipboard in his work-worn hands. He sported a light beard and a mesh cap with the hardware store name on the front. He was not large, but he was built like a man who lifted and carried things for a living.

Styx's sour mood disappeared. He turned on all the charm. "Mr. Davis? Good afternoon. You got a minute to talk to us about those sweet wheels you got on display up front?"

"These are the boys I was telling you about." The salesman's voice followed us.

We shook hands with Mr. Davis. The owner was happy to chat us up about the Grasshopper.

"It belonged to your son?" Styx said, patting the moped's seat.

"Yup," Mr. Davis said. "Bought it for him for high school graduation."

"Wow." I wondered what it would be like to have such a cool dad. "He must've loved it."

Mr. Davis made a soft, sad sound. "Wasn't ever good enough for him. He wanted a Harley." The man shook his head. "Well, he's got one now."

Styx nodded. "Lucky for us, I suppose. We'd sure like to take this one off your hands. I can assure you, we'll enjoy and appreciate it."

"Not like my ungrateful son, you mean?" Mr. Davis barked a laugh. "Never been sure what to do with that boy."

Styx commiserated. "Fathers and sons, right? What are you gonna do?" I swear he looked at me for a second when he said it. To Mr. Davis he said, "I got a good joke for you."

"Bring it."

"Why is the first story in the Bible about Adam and Eve and the second story about Cain and Abel?"

"Why?"

"'Cause Adam and his sons still won't talk about their problems."

Mr. Davis hooted. Styx stuck out his palm and they slapped. We all grinned at each other.

"You want the bike? Make me an offer," Mr. Davis said.

"This is a blessing in disguise," Styx said. "We're low on cash, but we can offer you a trade."

"Trade for what?" Mr. Davis's expression faded from friendly to skeptical.

"The perfect thing," Styx assured him. "The thing you want most."

The old guy snorted. "And what's that?"

Styx's smile dazzled us. It was almost like a starburst flashed from the corner of his teeth, like the cartoon dad on the candy cigarette box.

"You can't give me what I want most," Mr. Davis said, staring at the Grasshopper. "And you're too young to see that."

Styx stayed confident. "Hold the moped for us. We'll come back within the week. Make you an offer you can't refuse."

✦ ✦ ✦

"How do you know a lawn mower is what Mr. Davis wants most?" Bobby Gene asked, the second we hit the sidewalk, carrying the tube of rust remover.

"The lawn mower's not going to work," Styx said. His cloak of charm slipped off, and he fell quiet again.

"What?" I said when he didn't continue. "But that's all we have."

"We need another trade," Styx said. "The lawn mower for . . . something."

"What does Mr. Davis want most?" I asked.

Styx glanced sideways at me. It was a few moments before he answered. "We'll work something out."

We were feeling upset, so we splurged on a trip to the diner. We ordered a whole mess of chicken strips and three large milkshakes. Vanilla for me, strawberry for B.G. and coffee with caramel for Styx. I regretted my order as soon as I heard Styx's. I couldn't have asked for anything plainer.

The waitress saw Styx slip his candy cigarette from his pocket. "No smoking," she said.

Styx snorted. "It's fake." He twirled the candy cigarette over his place mat.

"It's policy," she said, like she didn't get it.

"Sure thing, Janine." Styx studied the name badge on her chest for a while. "Pretty clearly fake, but it passes."

The waitress crossed her arms over her stomach. Her voice got tight. "Anything else I can get you?"

Styx teased the candy cigarette between his lips. "We're good," he said.

She spun away in a huff. She was being weird and so was Styx. I didn't see what the big deal was. The candy cigarette was like an extension of Styx's fingers. I barely noticed anymore.

Janine returned a few minutes later with our order. She

slammed the plates down on the table in front of us and marched off.

"Hey," Styx called after her. She looked over her shoulder. "Sorry," he said. "Sorry. I— Honestly. Sorry." He held up the candy cigarette and made a show of dropping it back in his pocket.

She nodded and left.

We dug in. Chicken strips, fries and a milkshake is about the best meal in the world.

"Not bad," Styx commented as he sipped the shake. "About as good as you find in Indy." He shook his head. "Best fries in the city were around the corner from my house."

"You lived in Indy?" Bobby Gene said. "Not just visited?"

"Yeah." Styx shrugged. "We lived a lot of places."

"You and Pixie?"

Styx said nothing.

"How come you move so much? Where'd you live before Sutton? How come you're in a foster home anyway?" Bobby Gene poured questions into the silence like a hose stuck on full blast.

Styx shook his head.

"You don't wanna know about that stuff," he said finally.

"But—"

I nudged Bobby Gene to shut up. Foster home? Maybe so. But his prying was going to get us in trouble in a minute.

Styx had a teakettle expression on his face, like steam was filling up his head. He sucked hard on his straw, gnawed a trio of fries. Then he tore a chicken strip in half with a grunt like the Hulk.

Bobby Gene nudged me back. He got annoyed with me when I did that, because it usually meant I could see or understand something he couldn't.

Styx wasn't being his usual cheerful self. It gave me a tight feeling in my stomach that had nothing to do with being hungry or full.

"We like you," I told Styx. "That's why he wants to know. He didn't mean anything by it."

"You guys are all right too," Styx answered. He snagged a fry and swiped it through ketchup. "But if anyone asks, I never said that."

I copied his movement exactly. "I didn't hear anything."

# CHAPTER 23

## PORCHES AND PROMISES

With Styx's charm set on low, we were no longer fearless adventurers. We became three boys too far from home.

It was a relief to arrive back in our own woods. We fetched the lunch box and sat under the trees with it. Styx was still in a bit of a mood.

It fell to me to be the impossibly charming one, so I leaned in to practice my Styx-craft. "This one time," I told him, "we brought a couple of frogs to church. We had them in our shirt pockets. In the middle of the sermon, one of them got the Holy Ghost and started leaping around and croaking all over the altar."

"Just one of them?" Styx said.

"Yeah, it was my frog that went nuts," I said. "The reverend called it the Lord God in action through nature. 'Wake!' he yelled out to the whole congregation."

Bobby Gene laughed. "The other one stayed quiet in my pocket the whole time. Real prayerful."

"No way," Styx said.

"Yes, way," Bobby Gene confirmed. "You're not the only one with wild stories."

"Tell me another."

I thought about it. "This one time, we took a jar of lightning bugs into the grocery store . . ."

Styx puffed on his candy cigarette and scrubbed at the lunch box like it was going to save his life. It was gentle and tedious work. His long fingers danced with the rag against the metal. He massaged each hinge lovingly as I regaled him with the best stories I could think of from our entire lives up until now.

Finally Styx raised his head. "Check it out."

The lunch box was clean. It wasn't as perfect as a new one, but it had character. Kinda like the beat-up old furniture Mom liked that we weren't supposed to call old.

"Is it an antique?" Bobby Gene said, reading my mind.

It had a faded blue and red picture on it. A cartoon man flying with his fists forward and a cape streaming behind. The telltale *S* on his chest.

"It's a bird, it's a plane . . . ," Bobby Gene said.

"It's Superman!" we chorused.

"Is it valuable?" I ran my finger over the image. The

lunch box looked like it might have been awesome . . . when it was new.

"It's worth enough," Styx said. "Some people are into this kind of thing."

✦ ✦ ✦

Styx stayed for dinner, then we hung out on the back porch as the sun went down. Lightning bugs flicked across the yard, teasing each other with their taillights. We lounged in the chaises, shooting the breeze. And then Styx got kinda quiet again.

"Listen," he said. "We need to make moves on this motor, right?"

"Is now the best time to talk about it?" I pointed up to the open window screens. Dad was watching TV pretty loud, but you never knew how sound might carry.

"We can talk tomorrow," Styx agreed. "I just don't think we should put it off anymore."

Had we been putting it off? We'd only just gotten the lunch box ready. But Styx hadn't seemed to be in a big hurry until today.

"Pond trip tomorrow?" I suggested.

"Sure thing," Styx said. "If it's hot like today, that'll feel good."

Bobby Gene and I glanced at each other. Awkward. How to tell Styx we weren't allowed to swim?

Mom poked her head out the door, sparing us. "Wrap it up, boys."

"Aww," we chorused. It wasn't even totally dark yet. The cruel reality of summer was that bedtime often preceded actual dark.

"Good night, Styx," Mom said, in a tone as clear and final as the end-of-school-day bell. She balanced Susie with one arm and waved the other hand over the dessert dishes surrounding us. We were meant to clean up and follow her, and Styx was meant to go home.

But Styx, not having a mom of his own and all, was never one to pick up on these things. He flopped back onto the chaise and wiggled his butt into the cushion, getting comfy. He crossed his arms behind his head.

"The night is young, Mrs. Franklin," he said.

"And so are you," Mom answered. "It's near bedtime."

"We have to go in," I whispered to Styx. "That's her pre-punishment voice."

He glanced at me with clear disdain for my rule-following. "If that's how you want to roll," he said.

It wasn't how I wanted to roll. Of course it wasn't. But Styx didn't understand the pressure we were under.

"Say good night," Mom ordered.

"Good night, Styx," we said.

Mom herded us inside. There was no use complaining. She put Susie in her high chair, then handed us each a cup of water in the kitchen. We were always required to hydrate after being outside, especially in the summer.

She leaned her hips against the counter, crossed her arms and stared at us. We stood on the tile in our bare feet, slugging down the cool, smooth water. They were big cups. Mom was on to something with the water thing. No matter how squirrely we felt when we burst in the door, by the time we'd chugged it all down we were looking pretty docile.

Over the rims of our cups, we watched her watching us. Uh-oh.

"Okay, guys, we need to have a little talk." Her tightly crossed arms and eagle-eye stare said plenty.

We lowered our cups and waited. From the living room came the low, familiar sound of the TV news. I tried to take comfort in that. The impending "talk" was not serious enough for Dad to be involved.

Or else, so serious that it was better for Dad not to know. I gulped.

"You've been spending a lot of time hanging out with Styx lately, haven't you."

"Not that much, really," I said, at the same time as Bobby Gene said, "Oh, yeah, he's great."

We glanced at each other.

"Only sometimes," I rambled on. "In the afternoons, a little bit. We have our chores with Cory in the morning and all. We've been real faithful about that."

"Styx is a troubled boy," Mom said.

"How come you don't like him?" Bobby Gene said.

"I didn't say I don't like him. He's very charming."

This is what Mom says about people she doesn't really like.

"It sounds like he's had a hard life, is all. Sometimes that makes people a little rough around the edges."

Styx was rough around the edges, for sure. He did what he felt like. He saw everything and calculated all the angles. What would Styx say, right now, to Mom?

"We're trying to be good neighbors," I said. "You wouldn't want us to turn our backs on someone just because he's had a hard time, would you?"

Mom's lips tightened. She didn't want to have to disagree with that.

"He doesn't really have a family," I explained. "He's all alone and he's new here. We can help him, you know? Be a good influence and stuff."

Surely that wasn't even stretching the truth too far. Styx was learning all kinds of stuff from us, just like we were learning all kinds of stuff from him.

Mom uncrossed her arms. "I need you to know I have some concerns, that's all."

Bobby Gene sighed, his feet twitching toward the hallway. "Can we go?"

"Okay," Mom said. "Caleb," she added as Bobby Gene went tearing off to our room. I lingered so she could say whatever she had to say that my brother wasn't likely to understand. "You know what I mean, right, sweetie? About Styx?"

I shrugged. "Yeah, I guess." Even though, no, I really didn't.

"If you play with him, I need you to be careful."

"We're always careful."

Mom bent and kissed my face. "It's still my job to remind you."

"Yeah, yeah." I wiped away the spot as if she'd slobbered on me like Susie would.

✦ ✦ ✦

"Styx wouldn't have let Mom push us around like that." I was griping so loudly, Bobby Gene started patting the air to quiet me down.

"When it's Mom, it doesn't count as pushing us around," he said.

"Still."

We had LEGO pieces out strewn around the room. We were pecking through the piles, looking for all the green and black ones. We were going to build a scale model of the moped.

Bobby Gene scooped up a handful of pieces and made a LEGO waterfall through his fingers. "Styx is good for dealing with people like Cory, but he really doesn't get what we're up against around here."

"How great would it be to have no parents?" I fantasized as we got into bed. "To do whatever the heck we wanted, anytime."

"Yeah," Bobby Gene agreed. "Except then one of us would have to get a job or something."

He was harshing my vibe with his practicality.

"Forget about that part. I'm talking midnight Rice Krispies candy. Ice cream for breakfast."

"TV all night until the sun comes up?" Now he was getting into the spirit.

"Twenty-four-hour video game marathon."

"Pizza for every meal."

"No news, only our shows."

"No vegetables."

We kept on making the list until we couldn't keep our eyes open. "No parents would be the coolest," Bobby Gene mumbled. He slid into a half snore.

"Yeah . . ." I drifted away too.

One last thought slipped through my mind. Styx's face, on the sidewalk earlier.

"Hey, Styx, you ever ride in a limo?"

"Once."

# CHAPTER 24

## ORIGINAL

The next afternoon we scarfed down our lunch in record time.

"Time to go fishing," Bobby Gene announced. We scooted out of the house while Mom had Susie still bunched up in the high chair. We grabbed up our poles and hiked through the woods to see if Styx wanted to come along.

Styx and Pixie were waiting for us at Styx's office.

"What's she doing here?" Bobby Gene took the words right out of my mouth.

"I beg your pardon," Pixie said. "I'm brightening up the place, don't you think?"

Her skirt had reflective sparkly things all over it. So technically, yes, she was brightening up the place.

"We only have three poles," Bobby Gene said, as if that kind of logic was going to deter her. I mean, this was a person who owned *multiple* headbands with ears. Today they were tiger-striped cat ears.

It didn't escape my notice that both Styx and Pixie had beach towels slung over their shoulders.

On the way to the pond, Pixie was less enamored with the mermaid tree than I expected. I made a point to show it to her and everything. It seemed like the sort of thing a girl might like.

But she only shrugged. "I want to see the water."

So much for that.

Pixie stood on the shore of our pond and declared it good. "It's an oasis," she said. "A place that revives weary travelers and gives them strength for the rest of the journey."

An oasis. I liked that.

"What's its name?" she asked.

"The pond? Uh, I don't think it has one." I glanced at Bobby Gene.

He shrugged. "We just call it the pond."

Pixie frowned. "Unacceptable. Everything this good should have a name."

"I guess we can come up with one for it," I suggested.

Pixie looked us up and down. "I don't know if you can be trusted with that kind of power," she said. "Naming is a very big deal."

We took off our shoes right away. There was barely

room for all four of us up on the log. I got tucked between Styx and Pixie, our legs dangling over the brook. Her toenails had sparkly polish.

It was probably only a matter of time before Styx or Pixie would suggest we swim. Now there were four of us. That seemed like a drown-proof number. (Mom would not agree, of course, but Mom wasn't here.) I was feeling okay about the possibility.

Styx brought up a fishing pole and studied the winding mechanism.

"Ahhh, Styx!" Pixie squealed as the other end of the pole bounced around in her face.

"My bad," he said with a grin. He tossed the pole back to the shore.

"How'd you end up with a cool name like Styx?" Bobby Gene asked.

"I'm named for a river," he said.

"A river around here?" The only river I knew the name of around here was the Wabash, but I'd like to see a river called Styx.

"It's from Greek mythology," Styx said.

"The river of death," Pixie said, in her very un-deathlike voice.

"Yeah, it's the river you have to cross to get to the underworld. You gotta put pennies in the ferryman's hands to get you across it."

That sounded awesome.

"What kind of people name a kid after the river of death?" Bobby Gene blurted out. I gave him a side-eyed glare. Sometimes he didn't know any better than to put his foot in it.

Styx raised a shoulder. "The same kind that don't stick around."

"I'm named after our dad," Bobby Gene reminded everyone. Then helpfully added, "And Caleb's named after nobody."

"Thanks a lot," I said.

He looked at me. "Well, you're not."

Maybe it was best to change the subject. "So this motor? What's the deal there?"

Styx nodded. "We need a whole day, is the problem."

"But we still have another week of chores with Cory."

"Yeah. But the motor we can trade for is a ways away, and there's some timing to consider. We have to leave in the morning, come back in the afternoon. No other way."

A whole-day adventure? Brilliant.

Pixie wrinkled her nose. "I will not be going on that trip," she said. "I'll be here at the unnamed oasis, if anyone needs me."

Styx continued, unfazed. "Can we get Cormier to cover for you?"

Bobby Gene looked skeptical. "It's risky."

"We can try," I said. "It would mean he'd get out of chores too."

"Or we can wait the week," Styx said. "Maybe it's not such a rush, you know?" He pointed his face to the sky and breathed in sunshine.

"The sooner we get it, the sooner we can ride," I said. I had my mind set on the museum, after all.

"True."

It was funny. Sometimes Styx acted all intense about it, like the trade was everything. Other times it was all, let the good times roll and we'll work it out in the end. He could be chill like that. Real smooth. And it was easy to be lulled by Styx's tide. Easy to forget the taste of Dissatisfied. Ordinary.

But it wasn't going to go away.

Unless I made it. Time to be the new me. Brash and bold and taking the world by storm, that was Caleb Franklin for you.

I pushed my feet down until they touched the water. The cold felt good. "So are we going to swim, or what?"

"Heck yeah," Styx said. He stripped off his shirt and jeans, revealing a pair of gray boxers underneath. He balance-beamed across the log and climbed onto the mound of rocks at the far edge of the water.

Then he dove straight in. Like a madman! Lesson one of natural water: never dive in blind.

Styx surfaced in the middle of the water. "This is great,"

he called. "Come on in." He wasn't really that far away, but it was like he'd entered another world.

To my surprise, Bobby Gene followed him. Not with a fancy, splashy dive, but a slow ease, up to his ankles, then his shins. He bent and touched the water with his hands.

"We can be the lifeguards, if you want," Pixie said. Maybe she sensed my hesitation.

"Nah." If Bobby Gene was going in, there was no way I was missing out. Styx might've been the first in the water, but it had been my idea to swim.

Pixie and I climbed down from the log. We stood on the shore long enough to strip out of our surface clothes. Under all the sequins, it turned out that Pixie had on a proper bathing suit. My shirt landed easy against my shoes. My shorts—

I hesitated. I didn't have a bathing suit. Or boxers like Styx. Mine were run-of-the-mill tighty whities. Except they had blue bands at the top, so Mom could tell mine apart from Bobby Gene's.

"Oasis Pond," I said. "Maybe you already named it."

"Yeah," Pixie said. "That suits it. Are we going in?"

"Don't look."

She shielded her face with one hand. I pulled off my shorts. Pixie eased her sparkly toes right up against the fishing poles, where we'd left them lying on the shore. "Hmm," she said.

I rushed into the water, dipping straight past the reluctant Bobby Gene. I kept going until my underwear was covered.

"Okay," I called.

Pixie entered the water as daintily as you might expect of someone who routinely wears tutus.

"Hmm." She lay back and her hair fanned out against the water.

"What?" I asked.

"I think I've put my finger on why you're not very successful fishermen."

Oh. Ha. "Don't you mean you put your toes on it?"

Pixie smiled at the sky. "Indeed."

I grinned, kicking my legs up. "Someday we're gonna catch something. Really. Someday we might even put the poles in the water."

We laughed.

"Are there even fish in here?" Pixie asked.

Bobby Gene's voice floated from above. "We've never seen any." He splashed around in the shallows.

"Why did you get the nickname Pixie?" I figured it was okay to ask since we'd been talking about names earlier.

"I picked it out."

"Why?"

"I have a brother now. I thought we should match."

It took me a while to work it out. Pixie and Styx. Pixie Styx?

"You're a freak," I informed her.

"I'm *original*." She enunciated each syllable.

"Freak."

She grinned, as if she knew that secretly I was thinking: No one would ever call Pixie "ordinary."

"What?"

She grinned wider. "Shut up," she said. "You know you like me."

"Shut up," I said. Because I did.

The sudden awkward feeling between us was covered by a splash. Styx climbed out of the water and back onto the rocks. "Starfish!" he called out. I spun in time to see him toss himself, spread-eagle, into the sky above us.

His dive lasted forever. He hovered, as if he'd flapped some unseen wings.

I held my breath. There was no boundary he couldn't touch, no field off-limits, no end to what was possible.

Styx Malone knew how to fly.

# CHAPTER 25

## MODEL BEHAVIOR

"I wonder how much gas it would take to go all the way to Chicago," I said. In my mind's eye, we were zipping along the highway already, weaving in between cars like the Fast, or the Furious.

"Too far," Bobby Gene said. "Won't get back in time for dinner."

"Okay, Indy, then. The museum." I scratched at the seam between two flat green LEGO pieces. We were working on the Grasshopper model. We'd had to redo and scale it down when it turned out we didn't have nearly enough green and black pieces.

"Even Indy's pretty far," Bobby Gene answered. "But it's fun to imagine."

Imagine? Only for now. Soon it would be possible, in the real world. With Styx, all things were possible. My mind ticked, twisting itself into knots with all the possibilities. Everything was shiny, golden, before my eyes.

Bobby Gene sat cross-legged, lining up black pieces in the shape of a rear tire. I lay on my stomach, sifting through the green pieces, pulling out all the onesies and flats.

We were early enough in the redesign process that we were working with the door open. We didn't try to cover it up when Mom barged in.

"Boys, I need you to take out the trash."

We were soul-deep in the planning stage. We had achieved the kind of intense, shared-vision mind-meld that involved a lot of "Ooh-ooh, what if we . . ." and "Oh, yeah, that's genius" kinds of revelations. We were on another plane. No quibbling, only shorthand. Boom, boom. We were rocking it. Mom didn't know what she was interrupting.

"Caleb, did you hear me? Trash."

"We'll pencil it in for after supper," I answered. The LEGO pieces clattered against each other, making a satisfying sound as I sifted.

Total silence from on high. Total. The kind that pulls the hum out of the light sockets. I swiveled to meet Mom's icy glare. Her eye lasers stabbed me with shivers.

"Excuse me?" she said.

Bad mistake.

Bobby Gene sucked air through his teeth, a small

desperate whistle. "We're going. Going now." He scrambled to his knees.

"Naw." I doubled down on the stupid. "We're in the middle of something, Mom. Why you gotta jam us up like this?"

"Caleb Franklin, if you don't get up off that floor right this minute and do what I'm asking of you . . ."

Bobby Gene was already up. "It's cool, Mom. We got this. We got this." He grabbed my arm and hissed, "It'll take two seconds."

Mom's laser eyes continued to lop off my body parts. How did she expect me to take out the trash with no arms?

Bobby Gene tugged me up. We hustled past her and pulled the kitchen trash.

"Dude," Bobby Gene said. "That was close. We almost got grounded or something in there. You realize that, don't you?"

He was right, of course. But for some strange reason, I didn't even care.

"Styx does whatever he feels like," I reminded him. "Why can't we?"

Bobby Gene gaped at me. "You're kidding, right?"

I was still half in the mind-meld. Where all that mattered was the Grasshopper. My mind soared as if it was ours already. The ability to do whatever we wanted. To write our names on the map in giant swooping letters. To say we were here. We came, we saw, we conquered, and we lived to tell the tale.

If Bobby Gene hadn't been there to stop me talking back to Mom, I don't know what might have happened.

It was like I'd breathed something mind-altering. The fantasy was going to my head.

✦ ✦ ✦

Cory Cormier was all that stood in the way of us getting a free day to go get Styx's motor. But convincing him to cover for us turned out to be not so easy.

"How come you won't tell me why?" he kept saying.

"We have business to take care of," I told him. "With Styx."

"Business?" He perked up a little at that, but just as quickly his expression soured. "Oh, that guy. He's still hanging around?"

"He's our friend," I said. "Don't knock him."

"What's in it for me?" Cory said. "If I cover for you."

"A day free of chores, duh," Bobby Gene said. "We could all use a day off."

Cory considered it. "I need more than that. If we get caught, it's all of us on the line."

Stalemate. We didn't have much else to offer him.

I wasn't giving up. The Grasshopper dream was still alive in my head. The buzz of the engine grew louder and louder and louder. . . .

"Caleb." Bobby Gene grabbed my arm and yanked me out of Cory Cormier's driveway. A Harley chopper zoomed up and parked right in front of us. A huge bear of a guy, clad head to toe in leather, swung off the motorcycle.

"Hi, Uncle Greg," Cory said.

"Hey, squirt." They slapped hands. "Who are your friends?"

"This is Caleb and Bobby Gene."

"That's an impressive ride," I said.

"Thanks," he said. But he wasn't really interested in us. "Your mom home?"

"Yeah," Cory said.

"Later, kid." Uncle Greg trooped into the house.

So it was true. Cory had an uncle, and he sure looked like he belonged in a motorcycle gang. "I always thought you made him up," I said offhand. Not the brightest thing to say when we needed a favor, but no one's perfect.

Cory glared at me. "Well, I didn't. *Bye.*" He stomped toward the house.

"Way to go," Bobby Gene muttered.

"Shut up."

We rode home, dejected. We'd never get Cory to agree to our terms. We might need to have Styx come back and mediate. Or else getting away for a whole day might never be possible. Letting Cory in on our full plan was out of the question.

"We could wait him out," Bobby Gene suggested. "We only have a week of chores left."

"Styx says we need to move on it," I said. "Aren't you tired of waiting?"

Bobby Gene thought about it. "If we don't get the Grasshopper soon, we won't have much time to ride before school starts."

All the more reason to make this happen. Stat.

We'd have to come up with something to give Cory what he wanted. Something that didn't give away our entire plan.

# CHAPTER 26

## GONE

We had no choice but to report our failure to Styx. We'd have to come up with another plan to get a whole day free. Or else wait until our sentence was over. But I didn't want to wait, and I knew Styx wouldn't either.

We tromped through the woods to meet Styx and Pixie for another afternoon at the pond. I needed another dose of the fearless, flying Styx.

How would Styx have handled Mom last night? I knew he could've got by without ever touching a trash bag. And what would he have said to Cory to get him on our side? He'd have gotten it done right the first time. I still had a lot to learn.

Styx was waiting for us at his office with three towels. Smoking a candy cigarette. Alone.

"Where's Pixie?"

"Gone," Styx said, his voice heavy.

"Gone where?" Bobby Gene asked.

"I thought she knew we were coming. We had plans." I was more disappointed than I ought to be.

"*Gone* gone. DCS gone. They came and took her." Styx drew on his candy cigarette, in the way that meant he had a lot of thoughts he wasn't going to say.

"Who came?" Bobby Gene asked.

"The suits. DCS."

That had a bad ring to it. "So . . . we'll see her tomorrow?" I asked.

"Not likely," Styx said. "She's gone."

I frowned. "What are you talking about?" Something uncomfortable stirred inside me.

Bobby Gene touched my shoulder. "I think he means she got moved to a new foster home."

"Why? How? Who would do that?" I stretched, trying to see through the woods toward the house. All I saw was leaves and branches.

Styx raised a shoulder. "No rhyme or reason."

"But—"

"Look, it's hard to understand when you've got it good like you two. So let's drop it, okay?"

*Have you met me?* I wanted to ask. I didn't know how to let go of anything. Not till I had it all figured out.

"But you said shc was your sister."

Styx shrugged. "She is. We had a good run. For a second there . . ." His voice trailed off and he tapped the candy cigarette against his lips. "Anyway, let's get this show on the road, right?"

He stalked off toward the pond.

We scrambled after him, juggling the three poles and our catch bucket between us. "But . . . won't you miss her?"

"She's a pain more than anything," Styx said. "Always getting in my stuff."

To be fair, Bobby Gene and I didn't have firm legs to stand on in this conversation. We'd tried to trade our sister, after all. But that was different. The idea of someone taking her away against our will . . . that made me feel all squeamy inside.

"Let me tell you how it is," Styx said, his voice as scratchy as gravel. "Doesn't matter who you miss. Put her out of your mind. You'll never see her again."

"But—"

Styx grabbed up one of the fishing poles from Bobby Gene and kept walking. "Only person you can ever count on is yourself."

There were lots of people I could count on. Bobby Gene. Mom. Dad. Styx. Even Susie could be counted on, at least for a good snuggle.

But I got what Styx was saying. Freedom came with a price.

✦ ✦ ✦

We circled the pond and sat on the taller edge of the rocks. It wasn't really a cliff, but with Styx around it sure felt like one. Our legs dangled down against the mossy rocks.

We were only a few feet higher above the water than usual, but the view was entirely different. Maybe we needed that today.

From here, we could start jumping, flying, soaring to infinity. Any moment now, the magic might hit. Take us to that other place. The Styx place, where a smile is like money and it never ever rains.

Styx was quiet for a time. But with us around he had to know that wasn't going to last.

"So, Styx," I said, real casual. "What's with the candy cigarettes?" Before today, it had been a while since I'd seen him with one, come to think.

Styx fake-puffed. "Real cigarettes are too expensive," he said. "And smoke in your lungs is no good for you."

"Yeah," Bobby Gene said. "Yuck."

"Right. So why even do it at all?"

Styx shrugged. "I like sugar?"

"Nah, you could just eat all kinds of candy, then."

"You got me there." Styx turned thoughtful for a minute. Finally he said, "There's something cool about smoking, don't you think?"

We shook our heads.

"I think it's mostly gross," Bobby Gene said.

"Yeah . . . I don't know how to explain it." Styx stared into the butt end of the little white stick. "I like to pretend it's burning, you know? A little flame that I can hold in my hand. There's some kind of power in that."

We kicked our legs into the air over the pond.

I forgot about the question. Out of nowhere, Styx added, "It's like building a bonfire to burn up all the things you hate. Except tiny, and all the time."

"Dad builds a bonfire in the summer sometimes," I said. "We can ask him to do one."

"Sure," Styx said. "That'd be all right."

"We roast hot dogs and marshmallows," Bobby Gene said. "S'mores."

My stomach started rumbling. "Maybe we can do it tonight," I said. "How have we not had s'mores yet?"

"Some more what?" Styx asked.

Bobby Gene and I stared at him. "S'mores."

Styx stared back.

"Oh, heck no," Bobby Gene said. "We gotta fix you up right now."

# CHAPTER 21

## BLAZE OF GLORY

Dad helped us build the good kind of fire, the kind where the logs make a square on all sides and you can keep building it and building it, throwing on new logs and crisscrossing them over. Flames as bright as daylight, where you have to stand back from the heat.

Styx seemed impressed by the size of the fire, and even more impressed by the full spread of hot dogs and fixin's on the picnic table. Mom had gone all out. Three packs of hot dogs, a pile of buns to match. Two bags of chips—barbecue and regular. Plus she had laid out every kind of condiment you could imagine—onions, relish, shredded cheese, bacon bits—which was weird because Bobby Gene and I were ketchup and mustard all the way. Meat and sauce was what we lived for.

When Cory Cormier came strolling up across the lawn,

it was all I could do to stop myself from blurting out "What are you doing here?" I forgot. Mom had called his mom and invited him. Like we needed a playdate or something. We were already seeing the guy every day.

"You're doing all this work together. It's nice to make time for each other as friends," Mom had said. And truth be told, I guess that's what we were now. Friends? With Cory Cormier? Stranger things had happened.

Or perhaps this was evidence of how badly Mom wanted us not hanging out with Styx every day.

"Hey, Cory," we said.

He sn.iled at us. "Thanks for inviting me." He had a pack of marshmallows in his hand. "My mom sent these."

Perfect. You could never have too many marshmallows at a campfire. We added them to the food table.

"This looks awesome," Cory said.

Dad strolled over and clapped his hands. "Welcome, gents, to the Franklin Fire Festivities!"

Oh, man. Bobby Gene and I rolled our eyes. Dad looked pretty happy, though. It was hard to be embarrassed by him.

He waved his hands like a magician revealing the table, which was in plain sight. "Step right up to the smorgasbord."

We grabbed up plastic plates and then, out of nowhere, Bobby Gene remembered his manners. "Styx, would you like to go first?"

"Uh, yeah, okay." Styx took a bun and opened it up on

his plate. He glanced with uncertainty toward the packs of cold hot dogs.

"See, what you do is you get the bun all ready, with your condiments and stuff," I said. "Then you roast the dog and plop it right in there. Ready to go."

Styx moved toward the ketchup area. Cory went next. We all doctored our buns. Then we claimed chairs around the circle by placing our plates on the seats. They were those canvas camping chairs with a cup holder in the arm. Mom had ice-cold pop cans waiting for us in each slot already.

We trooped back to the table for the hot dogs themselves.

Then, to our eternal embarrassment, Mom pulled one of her Mom switcheroos.

"Please eat two carrots apiece," she said, lifting the lid off a casserole. This was an order, and basically the price of admission, as she was holding the hot dog roasting sticks behind her back as she spoke.

The carrots were fresh from the garden, crisp-steamed and sweet-buttered. Mom had left on the green stub of stalk, so they had little handles. They went down easy.

"Carrots, huh," Dad said. He snuck up behind Mom and slid one arm around her waist while the other went to work freeing a hot dog stick. He kissed her on the cheek. She smiled and winked at us.

"Ah-ah. You have to eat yours, too," Mom said in a scolding voice. "And so do I."

Dad's hands were full teasing her, but she managed to grasp two carrots and pop one into her own mouth and one into Dad's, much to his surprise. Mom, the kitchen ninja.

Dad laughed and crunched the carrot down until it resembled a cigar. "Well, boys, we lost this one. Carrots for all."

"Carrots for all is a win," Mom said. "Thank you." She doled out hot dog skewers, preloaded with two dogs apiece. How well she knew us.

We turned toward the flames.

Within minutes, one thing was perfectly clear: Styx Malone had never been to a bonfire before in his life.

# CHAPTER 28

## BONFIRE HEARTS

First, he inched toward the fire like it was going to jump out and burn him. The flames licked upward. He brandished his hot dog skewer at full arm's length, like a sword.

"Here, like this." I showed him how to put one foot up on the fire circle rocks and lean in to stick the hot dogs over the coals.

Bobby Gene and Dad liked to set their dogs straight flaming. I liked to rotate mine over a coal spot until they plumped up perfectly. Styx followed my motions exactly. Our dogs lined up side by side.

"And then you just wanna turn them every couple of minutes." I showed him. We rotated.

The big log at the center hissed with boiling sap. Its bark snapped and popped, causing a tremor in the flames. Awesome.

Styx flinched at the sound. He dropped his hot dog

skewer. It slipped, dogs first, straight into the cold ash at the edge of the fire circle.

"Man," he groaned, grabbing his head with both hands. "I lost 'em."

"They'll be perfectly fine," Dad said. He picked the skewer up out of the dirt and blew on it. "Just got a little nature on 'em."

Styx stared skeptically at them. "I'm cool," he said. "I'll eat the chips and stuff."

Dad frowned. "Nonsense." He thrust his own skewer toward Styx. "Hang on to that one." Dad marched over to the picnic table and slid Styx's ashy dogs right onto the wood. He took two fresh hot dogs out of the package, loaded them up and brought them back to Styx.

Styx reached for them, looking uncertain. "It's okay?"

It was hard to read Dad's expression, even though it was barely dusk. "I'll eat the ones that fell," he said. "Don't even worry about it."

"Huh." Styx sounded surprised.

Dad shrugged. "This one's easy to place on the scale. I can burn those germs right off."

"The scale?" Styx asked.

Bobby Gene and I groaned loudly. Here we were, enjoying a pleasant evening, and now Dad was about to launch into his positivity theory.

Dad flexed his shoulders as if to warm up for a sporting

event. "The scale of optimism to pessimism. Any problem you got, you gotta look for a way to keep it low on the scale."

That was enough explanation, really, but Dad was on a roll. A positive attitude is everything. Problem solving can be simple, blah, blah. It all sounded fine, sort of. Dad's way of making hard things seem easy, and complicated things seem simple. He thought it applied to everything, but I wasn't so sure.

Five minutes later, Styx's eyes were bugging out. "Okay, then. I get it."

Dad grinned. "Try to keep a hold on this batch, though. We don't have an unlimited supply."

Styx nodded. "Yes, sir." He gripped the skewer like a baseball bat.

We toasted the dogs right and scarfed them down. Styx ran his finger around the paper plate, licking up ketchup and potato chip flakes.

"You can have another hot dog," I told him. "As many as you want."

"Yeah?" he said. He smacked his lips, then glided toward the table like a hunter stalking his prey.

This time he did like Dad and piled a little bit of everything on it.

"Save some room for s'mores," Mom said.

"They say I've got a hollow leg," Styx reported around a mouthful of chips. He swallowed. "But I won't eat any more after this one."

Mom softened over him then. Styx wasn't going hungry, we knew, but hot dogs were a treat for all of us. I'd had three. Dad had had four—his two and Styx's dropped ones.

"You gave me a good excuse to tuck away a couple extra," Dad said, patting his stomach. "Thanks for that."

"It's no trouble, Mr. Franklin. I'm a good problem solver," Styx remarked. "These guys know."

We nodded. Surely Styx knew not to say anything about the escalator trade here.

Luckily Cory was busy tickling Susie's tummy. Coochie-coo. She gurgled for him. It would have been adorable if it hadn't been slightly sickening to watch.

We sat around the campfire until it was nothing but coals. There is no such thing as too many marshmallows. On a bonfire night in the middle of summer, bedtime is not a thing either. Except for Susie. Mom trucked her off to bed before the sky was fully dark. We settled into our camping chairs and planted our feet on the circle of stones. Styx's eyes glowed in the lapping of the flames.

There's no better thing to do around the campfire than tell stories. Styx was born for this. "Hey, Mr. Franklin. I ever tell you about the time . . ."

Within minutes, he had Dad laughing along with the rest of us. Amazing. They seemed to get along fine. Even though Styx told wild stories about things he'd seen and done, all the places he'd been, and to Dad, such adventures belonged in books, only to be whispered in the dark.

We saw the headlights when Mrs. Cormier showed up to get Cory. We said good night, and Dad walked him up to the car.

While they were gone, Styx said, "Listen. Cormier's still got a soft spot for the baby. Did you notice that?"

"I guess," Bobby Gene said.

"That's your ticket. Tell him he can have time with the baby if he'll cover for you."

"You think?"

The headlights faded and Dad's silhouette sloped its way back toward us.

"Trust me," Styx said. "It's a done deal."

When Dad finally went inside for good, he said, "Another half hour, boys, and then bed." He chucked Bobby Gene on the chin and rubbed the top of my head.

He stuck out his hand to Styx. Styx did that wary thing where he tucked his neck back and looked Dad up and down. Then he shook.

"Good to see you, Styx." Dad meandered up the lawn to the house. "You bank those coals when we call you in, you hear?"

"Yes, sir."

When he was gone, Bobby Gene threw on another log.

Dad liked to watch a fire simmer all the way down. We liked flames.

We sat quietly as the coals glowed in confusion beneath the new log. The edges of the fresh wood began to redden. Bobby Gene leaned forward and blew gently to rekindle the fire.

"Oh, yeah," said Styx. "That's what I'm talking about."

"Me too," I whispered. The coals versus the flames. I couldn't let myself settle and fade. Styx and I were flames.

Crickets chirped at us from the woods. Lightning bugs flashed against the black air, as if trying to compete with the fire, or with the stars. It was dark enough, and clear. We could see the swirl of the galaxy overhead.

"Your parents are cool," Styx said.

"What?" Bobby Gene practically choked. "They are wack."

"Nah." Styx shrugged and that was the end of that.

# CHAPTER 29

## LISA

Styx was right about Cory Cormier. The very mention of Susie made his whole face light up.

"Really? I can come play with her? You guys wouldn't mind?"

"Naw. We think it'd be real . . . special," Bobby Gene said.

"She likes you," I said. "Misses you, even."

"She does?" Cory scuffed his shoe against the ground. "I kinda thought so. Maybe."

"Course she does." I fist-bumped his shoulder. "Who wouldn't?"

Cory grinned. "It'll be good practice for me too."

"Practice?"

His grin got bigger. "I'm getting a baby cousin! That's what my uncle came over to tell my mom yesterday."

"Oh, congrats," Bobby Gene said.

"My mom has a bunch of my baby stuff in the attic that

he wants. Mom says I can make some things for the baby too. To help out."

"Help out?"

"Kids are expensive, Mom says. And Uncle Greg is pretty broke."

"How'd he get the stuff home on the motorcycle?" I asked, picturing him riding down Main Street holding a Pack 'n Play.

Cory shrugged. "He didn't take anything. He just picked stuff out. He's gotta buy a car now, Mom says. I say, no way he gives up the bike. You should see his house. It's decorated like Harley-Davidson central."

"Can't put a car seat on a chopper, that's for sure," Bobby Gene said.

This conversation was getting boring fast. "Well . . . that's great that you'll have a cousin."

"I'll teach her everything I know!" Cory declared. "Or him. We don't know if it's a boy or a girl."

"Anyway," I said. "A little Susie snuggle time . . . what's that worth to you? Worth covering for us for a morning?"

"Which morning?"

Soon, Styx had said.

"Tomorrow?"

Cory bit his lip and sighed. "Okay."

✦ ✦ ✦

We rushed through lunch so we could head to Styx's place. We were much too excited to report our news to wait until later.

We found Styx sitting on his back porch steps, but he wasn't alone. Some girl was with him. She was sitting right up next to him and smiling. He had his arm around her. Not around her shoulders, like buddy-buddy, but lower around her hip. His hand was almost all the way into her pocket, it looked like. Maybe he was reaching for some gum.

Their heads were close together. The girl had long brown hair and dimples. Her hair curtained across their faces as she leaned even closer toward him.

"Hey," we said.

Styx popped his head forward. "Hey."

"Hey," the girl said too, lifting her head. The curtain of hair shimmied back over her own shoulders, where it belonged.

"I thought we were meeting a little later," Styx said. "Did I lose track of time?"

The girl laughed softly and snuggled against Styx.

"We wanted to tell you something," I said. "It's pretty important."

"Let's do it later, okay?" Styx answered. "I'm a little busy, you know?"

"Sure, sure," Bobby Gene said. "No biggie."

Heck yeah, it was a biggie. "It won't take long," I told

Styx. I didn't want to say much more in front of the girl. "And we definitely have gum at our house, you know."

Styx looked confused.

We waited.

"Um, so, I'm Lisa," the girl said. "What are your names?" She said it in the kind of voice a new babysitter uses. As if we were little.

"Caleb," I mumbled.

"Bobby Gene."

"Hi, Caleb. Hi, Bobby Gene. It's really nice to meet you both," Lisa said. That's when I noticed she had her arm around Styx's waist too.

What was Styx doing hanging out with a babysitter? He was way too old to need one.

We waited.

"Guys," Styx said finally, "I'm gonna need a minute."

Bobby Gene's eyes got wide. "Oh—oh, right." He grabbed my arm and pulled me toward the woods.

"Hey," I complained.

"Catch you later," Bobby Gene said.

"Oh, they're so cute." Lisa giggled. "Your little brothers?"

"Yeah," Styx said. He could have corrected her, but he didn't.

I glanced back as Bobby Gene marched us away.

Brothers?

To be Styx's brother would be some kind of fantasy—nothing ordinary in that. But there was something else. Something about the way he claimed us. The way he said "Yeah," like he so often said "Yeah." It sounded different to me now. Slippery. He was letting her believe what she wanted to believe.

# CHAPTER 30

## SECRETS

Come morning, I was still reflecting on what Styx had said. And how he'd said it.

Today was the big day. Motor day. The adventure awaiting us was unclear, but we knew it would be one.

Little thoughts cropped up in my mind. Why, when the plan was so clear in Styx's mind, did it have to be so secret?

All along I'd liked the mystery. I liked taking each crazy dive into the world of Styx Malone. Why was my stomach doing somersaults now?

Bobby Gene and I muddled our way through breakfast, trying to tamp down our excitement. Soon enough we would know.

Sitting across the table from everyone felt the same as usual, but different.

We had a secret from Mom and Dad right now. And yet it didn't feel wrong. Styx made it sound like breaking the rules wasn't really so bad as long as you didn't get caught. That made a kind of sense.

I hung around afterward for a few minutes while Dad was reading the paper at the table. He hadn't gotten to the sports section yet.

"Hey, Dad?"

"Yeah?"

"How can you tell what someone's thinking?" I gripped the edge of the table and tugged till my fingertips paled. I had many more questions. Things I didn't know how to put in words.

"Did you try asking them?"

"What are you thinking?"

Dad turned a page in the newspaper and glanced at me. "I'm thinking this paper is full of bad news. I'm thinking of flipping to the funnies for a change."

"Is that it?"

"I s'pose not," he said. "I'm thinking about work. Thinking about you now. What's this about?"

I didn't know how to explain to Dad about Styx. At least, not in a way that wouldn't end with Dad forbidding us to hang out with him.

"Never mind," I told Dad. "I was just wondering."

"Well, okay, then." Dad pulled out the comics. "Here we go, that's better." He smiled at me.

For all the news he watched, it was funny how easily

Dad could let the whole wide world slip away. Four solid walls, a big-screen TV, and food on the table. Me and Bobby Gene doing all right in school. That was perfect to him. That was enough.

He was never going to tell me what I wanted to know. The questions in my heart were not ordinary.

"Thanks, Dad." I slid toward the hallway.

"Caleb?"

I turned back. "Yeah?"

"Sometimes you don't ever find out what someone else is thinking."

✦ ✦ ✦

Bobby Gene sat on the edge of his bed, pulling on his socks.

"You okay?" he said, glancing at me.

"Yeah." I took some socks and sat next to him.

"Hmm." He stuck his stocky legs straight out in front of him and tapped his toes together. I had to laugh.

Bobby Gene and I tell each other almost everything. And we know things we don't tell each other too. When he wakes up after an embarrassing dream, I know about it. I see him all hunched over, shuffling off to the bathroom. We always know who farted by the smell of it alone.

When I try to sneak more than my share of something, he can guess by the look on my face. We buy each other's

Christmas and birthday presents at the last possible minute so we don't accidentally give the surprise away.

Bobby Gene always seems to know when something's wrong with me. We know how to give each other space when we're out of sorts. Even when he's leaving me alone, we're always sort of together.

I can't imagine what it would be like not to have someone knowing all your business. To have real secrets.

Styx Malone had secrets.

# CHAPTER 31

## THE BEST-PREPARED HOBOS
## IN THE MIDWEST

"What's that?" Styx pointed to the brown paper sack in my hand. It had peanut butter sandwiches, baby oranges, packets of cheese crackers, and honey-roasted peanuts.

"You said we'd be gone all day," I said. "We might get hungry." Besides, we'd had to tell Mom we were going for a picnic lunch after chores. It would've looked odd if we hadn't taken any food.

"Why?" Bobby Gene asked. "Didn't you fill that up too?" He pointed to the lunch box in Styx's hand.

Styx frowned, but only said, "Good thinking." He pulled a large checkered bandanna from his back pocket. "I figured we'd forage for snacks, but this will do."

He took the sack from me, placed it in the middle of the cloth square and knotted the corners up in a bundle.

"Now we need a good stick," he said. We found one at

the edge of the woods, about two feet long, one inch thick, and still green enough to be slightly springy.

Styx shoved one end of the stick through the bandanna knot, then hiked the pack up over his shoulder, like a real old-timey hobo.

"What are we gonna do, hop a train and ride off into the sunset?" I joked.

"I hear the whistle blowin'," Styx answered. He handed me the stick and bundle to carry.

✦ ✦ ✦

Styx led us to the train yard, a part of town we didn't know. There wasn't anything you'd call a train station. Just a massive interchange of tracks. Sutton: the crossroads to nowhere. We weaved among rows of boxcars. Gray, brown, red, orange and green. Some had words on the sides. Others had letters or numbers. Some were rusty and ancient; some were shiny and new. Only a few doors stood open.

It was strangely easy. There were no guards. A few workers in neon vests ambled around the area. None of them seemed to notice us.

"This is the one we want," Styx said. "The ten-twenty-five always leaves from this track."

"These are all freight," Bobby Gene commented. "No passenger trains stop in Sutton." Mom said we had ridden on the train once, going up to Chicago for Aunt Cecily's wedding, way back before Susie was born. Before Dad drew a circle around Sutton in his mind. An electric fence, more like.

"Nah," said Styx. "This is way better."

A whistle blew.

"All aboard," Styx said. We climbed into an open green boxcar and settled crosslegged on the dusty floor. Whatever cargo had been in here had left sawdust all over everything.

The whistle blew. The metal rocked and chugged beneath us as the train began to move. My pulse pounded like drums against every inch of my skin.

Adventure, through and through.

The train pulled past the train yard onto a solo track across the farmland. The air stirred and sawdust whirled in tiny tornadoes beneath our knees.

"How far are we going?" Bobby Gene asked.

"How far do you want?" was Styx's answer.

Would we feel a jolt at the moment we crossed the town line out of Sutton? You could break right through an electric fence if you were strong enough to handle the current for a second. I held my breath.

As the train sped up, Styx moved to the doorway. He gripped the hand bar and leaned out.

"Styx Malone, you crazy fool!" Bobby Gene shouted. "Get back in here!"

Styx pulled himself back inside. Grinning. "Naw, man. You gotta try it."

The train chugged, past the backs of buildings and then out into the corn. Wind whipped past the door as the train picked up speed. We held on to the floorboards to keep from bouncing around.

"How do we get back?" Bobby Gene asked.

"Back?" Styx said. "Why would you want to go back?"

Bobby Gene's cheeks slackened.

"I'm kidding," Styx said. "Relax, homeboy." He leaned out the door again, barely gripping the hand bar with his fingertips, all his weight dangling by those thin wrists.

He threw his head back. "Woo! Y'all don't know what you're missing!" he shouted. He let go of one arm and stretched it into the whipping air.

Bobby Gene sucked in a sharp breath. To fall would be disastrous, but Styx would never fall.

"Come on." I scrambled to my feet. "Don't you want to try it?" The white of the sky and the chug of the train, the speed and the rocking and the grease scent tipped me toward giddy. I was close enough to touch Styx's magic.

Bobby Gene bit his lip, trying to look braver. We had been inseparable all our lives, but I was starting to see the difference between us. The way Styx challenged the world to a fight—it pulled me forward, leaving Bobby Gene behind.

"It's okay," I told him. "We're just having fun." I cuffed him on the shoulder where he sat with his arms crossed around his knees, watching the landscape. I went to the other side of the door, grabbed the hand bar tight and tossed my body into the wind, the way Styx had.

It hurt a little. My arms bore the whole weight of me as the metal lurched beneath me and I had to stretch through my toes to balance. The summer wind turned sharp and icy against my cheeks. I closed my eyes against the blur of clouds and treetops. My shirt billowed and pulled like a sail.

I drifted, free from all thoughts beyond *Don't let go!* The air wanted me, the ground wanted me, the circling gears below hungered to crunch my bones. My muscles strained to keep me in place—part boy, part machine, part nature.

It hurt more than a little.

I whooped, the way Styx had. Thick wind filled my mouth and throat, flapping my cheeks and drying my tongue. "Infinity, here we come!"

# CHAPTER 32

## DEAD MAN'S CURVE

"Okay, get ready," Styx said, brushing cheese-cracker crumbs from his fingers.

We'd been on the train for over an hour. The worry lines on Bobby Gene's forehead were looking more and more like Granddad Franklin's.

"Ready?" Styx said.

"For what?" Bobby Gene asked.

*For anything,* I thought.

"This is our stop." Styx tossed the last cracker wrapper back onto our paper sack. We rolled it all up into the bandanna.

Bobby Gene inched toward the open cargo door. He poked his head out past the edge, just enough to look around with one eye. "This doesn't look like a stop."

"It's not. But it's where we get off."

Bobby Gene moved back, placing himself between Styx and me. "Is it actually going to stop, though?"

"Trust me," Styx said. "It'll slow down enough."

Sure enough, the train began to slow.

"They call it Dead Man's Curve," Styx said.

"That's all kinds of comforting," Bobby Gene muttered.

"Ready?"

The train slowed to a crawl. Styx sat on the edge of the floor, his legs dangling out the door. Then he heaved himself out of the train. His feet skidded across the stones banking the tracks. He rolled into the grass, a soft landing.

"Awesome," I said, leaping after him.

My body hung in the grip of the wind for a long second before my feet touched down. Momentum carried me forward until I tumbled into the grass.

Bobby Gene inched toward the edge, his frown fully set. Styx and I got up and chased after the boxcar.

"Come on, B.G.," Styx said.

"You can do it. It's easy." My heart was still soaring, somewhere between earth and sky.

We trotted alongside the train. It was going slow enough that we could do that. But it would round the corner soon, and—

"Planning to ride off into the sunset, B.G.?" Styx said. "If you go to the end of the line, we'll be seeing you sometime tomorrow."

Bobby Gene scrambled to the boxcar's edge. "Don't leave me. Don't leave me!"

"Jump," I said. "It'll be okay."

Bobby Gene looked really scared. Maybe Styx and I should've left him at home for this one.

With a desperate cry, he finally did it. He rolled down the gravel bank and came to rest in the grass. Styx reached down and took his hand.

Bobby Gene brushed himself off.

"Looking good, B.G." Styx beamed. He raised his hand for a high five. Bobby Gene slapped it. Then he cut me an evil side-eye.

I swallowed the nagging feeling that maybe I wasn't being the best brother. Then again, Bobby Gene knew, like I did, that following Styx meant anything was possible.

✦ ✦ ✦

We walked through the fields, away from the tracks. We were smack in the middle of nowhere, USA. Nothing around for miles, apart from the occasional farmhouse in the distance. Much of the land was scrappy dirt, too uneven and rocky to farm.

We drew close to a ramshackle house and garage on a scrubby plot of land.

The low rail fence was much easier to climb than chain link. The lot inside it was peppered with junk. Someone did woodworking and metalwork here.

The house needed a paint job and the roof sagged. The large deck on the back looked weathered.

The garage had four big doors, two open. We walked right in.

Motors everywhere! Parts and tools and half-constructed machines. Lawn mowers, snowblowers, the shell of an old Ford pickup.

There was welding equipment and metal art. One wall of the garage was studded with every imaginable size of screwdriver and drill bit, wrench head, and plenty of things I didn't know the names of.

"This, here." Styx led us to a shelf stocked with dozens of lawn mower motors. "We're looking for a Briggs & Stratton model number 2307A." He showed us how to find the model number on each one.

"How'd you learn so much about motors, anyway?" I asked.

"I know a guy," Styx said.

"You know a lot of guys," Bobby Gene said.

We combed through the motors. Styx started at the top shelf. I started at the bottom, and Bobby Gene in the middle.

"What if there isn't one?" I asked.

"There will be." Styx sounded certain. "He always keeps

at least one of everything he might need. He's compulsive like that."

"Whose shop is this?" Bobby Gene asked.

Styx didn't answer right away.

"Let me guess," I said. "A guy you know."

Styx tapped his nose. "You're picking up what I'm putting down."

We combed through the motors. I lucked out and my finger landed on the right one first. "Found it!" I double-checked the numbers. Then Styx and Bobby Gene came and triple-, quadruple-checked it.

"Great," Styx said. "Wrap it up."

The motor was heavy. We wrapped it in the bandanna and tied it to the stick again, in the middle this time, not at the edge.

Styx carefully placed the lunch box in the spot where the motor had been, to complete the trade. "Okay," he said. "We're all set."

Bobby Gene carried one end of the stick and I carried the other, and we made our way back into the yard.

Boots thumped across the deck. "Hey," a man's gruff voice called. "What're you doing down there?"

# CHAPTER 33

## NARROW ESCAPE

The most notable thing about the old guy on the porch was that he was black, like us. Not what you expect in the middle of nowhere, Indiana.

Also notable: all the yelling.

He lumbered to the edge of the porch with a slightly bowlegged limp. "What do you kids think you're doing?"

"Uh-oh," Bobby Gene said. "Are we in trouble?"

No. "I thought we were allowed," I said.

"We are," Styx said. "It's just—"

That was all I needed to hear. I marched across the yard. "We're here finishing our end of a deal."

"Caleb, no!" Styx called after me. "Let's go."

"Ain't nobody making deals around here without my know-how." The man's voice was like a growl and a bark all at once. He squinted. "Styx?"

"Time to giddyup. Step on it, boys!" Styx's long-legged

stride drew him ahead of us. We puffed along behind him. The motor wasn't getting any lighter.

"Hey! You come over here."

We scooted across the yard, away.

"Damn it all, Malone. You know I can't chase you like that!"

We hefted the motor through the rail fence.

"I see you!" shouted the man. "Don'tchu go thinking I didn't see you! Ya hear?"

Our treasure . . . which might belong to someone else?

"We have to stop." Bobby Gene panted.

"Who is that guy?" I said. "Why are we in trouble? You said it was okay!"

Had Styx actually said it was okay? Had we asked?

My feet tried to catch up with my heartbeat. The uneven ground that had seemed interesting on the way in now seemed treacherous. We hustled.

"It is," Styx said. "We left our payment. Fair trade."

"That old lunch box?" I cried.

"I cleaned it up real nice," Styx said. "It's worth more than you think."

"We have to stop." Bobby Gene was out of breath.

Styx slowed. "We're good here," he said. The repair shop was growing smaller in the background. "He's not coming after us. Promise."

When we made it back to the spot where the tracks curved, we bent to catch our breath.

A train whistle blew.

"Here we go," Styx said. "Get ready."

The engine eased around Dead Man's Curve.

"Now what?" I asked.

"We get on."

"While it's moving?" Bobby Gene couldn't hide the terror in his voice.

"Sure," Styx said. "It'll be slow. It's even easier than getting off was."

He took the motor from us and began trotting alongside the train. After a moment, he hefted it into the car and swung himself up after it.

"Come on," he said. "See, not too bad." But he was practically a foot taller than us. He had more leg to work with.

Bobby Gene and I ran alongside the train, trying to figure out a plan.

Styx stuck his hand down and grasped my wrist. I held on to the doorjamb with my other hand and Styx heaved until I belly-flopped into the train car.

He should've done Bobby Gene first. I'm the better runner. And Bobby Gene was already out of breath from carrying the motor.

It took both of us to pull him in. By the time we got him off his feet, the train had started to speed up again. He lay with his legs hanging out of the train, clutching at me for dear life. I did my best to brace him while Styx reached down and lifted Bobby Gene's legs into the train.

"That was close," I said. Bobby Gene lay on the wood planks, catching his breath. I sat next to him, patting his back. I wanted him to know I was here. That I knew he was frightened and furious and didn't have the air to say so.

So I did it for him.

"What the heck did you get us into?" My breath came out in puffs of steam. It was cool in the shadows of the boxcar.

"Nothing," Styx said, patting the motor. "Done deal. We're cool."

"No way," Bobby Gene choked out. "We just stole from someone!"

"Oh, that's not the guy I made the arrangements with." Styx stayed smooth. "He doesn't run the place. We just didn't have time to waste on getting it all straightened out. We had a train to catch."

"What are you talking about?" I said. "It sure felt like we were in trouble."

"Nah. Trust me." Styx's eyes gleamed. "I wouldn't let anything like that happen to you guys."

Bobby Gene scooted closer to me. His gaze bounced between the motor and Styx and me. When he finally sat up, he spread himself like a wall in front of me.

We rode in silence. No joking, no stories. Nothing, apart

from the machinery chugging beneath us. This time, it wasn't lulling and steady. The wheels churned and churned, echoing with the scrape of metal on metal, the hiss of steam and the whine of brakes. The sounds were full with the sensation of slicing through land, the sense of forced progress, the sense that things made of steel would always win over things made of earth.

Bobby Gene's desperate, puffy breaths were loudest. I linked my arm with his. No matter what, no matter where, it was me and him.

No one knew where we were, or that we were extra passengers on this train.

Right then, we were a secret. Three freckles on the back of a metal snake. Invisible to the eyes of the world.

Styx stood with his shoulder against the open doorway, watching the landscape glide by faster and faster.

Styx could talk anyone into anything. Why hadn't we stayed and reasoned with the man? We could've left him with a smile on his face and one less motor in his collection. We could have walked away clean. What had Styx been thinking?

Dad's words from earlier floated back to me. *Sometimes you don't ever find out what someone else is thinking.*

Styx Malone had secrets.

Styx Malone told stories. Maybe they weren't always true.

# CHAPTER 34

## RIFT

We stashed the motor behind the same log where we'd hidden the wagon. By the time Styx and I got it tucked away, Bobby Gene was already walking toward the house.

Styx left me at the tree line. "Tomorrow we'll pop it into the lawn mower?" He fidgeted with his hands in his pockets.

"Usual time?"

Styx raised his chin. "Yeah?"

"Sure thing." Then I ran to catch my brother.

"Hi," Mom said as we staggered inside. "How was the picnic?"

Bobby Gene walked straight over to Mom and let her hug him. Uh-oh. This was way worse than I thought.

"Where have you been?" Mom patted his head. "You both look filthy."

"To the moon and back," I told her.

"Huh," Mom said. "I thought the astronaut phase was last summer. What happened to your international spy ring?"

"If we told you we'd have to kill you," I said.

"Right." Mom zipped her lip with two fingers. "Pretend I never asked. Go change and get washed up for dinner."

✦ ✦ ✦

We stood side by side at our sinks, scrubbing our hands. White soap bubbled up, then turned brown from all the train dirt. The water felt good; slipping, sliding away all the things I wanted to forget.

"Caleb—" Bobby Gene began.

"Don't." I held up a dripping hand to him.

"It seemed fun at first. But today was pretty scary."

"Scary COOL," I said. Now that we were back home, safe, it all felt awesome again. We'd hopped a boxcar like movie-star outlaws. We'd ridden toward the horizon. We were one step closer to the Grasshopper.

Bobby Gene stared pointedly at me. "We *stole*, Caleb."

"Styx says we didn't."

"And you believe him?"

"Well, yeah. Why shouldn't I?"

Bobby Gene sighed. "I don't think we should do this anymore."

Panic sliced through me. "We have to. We made a deal."

"We never said we'd lie, cheat, and steal."

"We haven't!"

Bobby Gene ticked off his fingers. "We lied to Mom. We cheated Cory. And now we—"

"Stole! Says you. Anyway, we didn't cheat Cory. We paid him."

"You know what I mean."

I whipped the hand towel at him. "We're about to achieve something awesome. We can't quit now!"

"How about being honest?"

"How about being fair?" I shot back. "Those fireworks were ours. Everything that comes from them belongs to us."

"And is our responsibility," Bobby Gene added.

"Exactly. We have to see it through to the end."

"Caleb—"

"B.G."

"Caleb."

"I'm meeting Styx tomorrow, whether you want to or not!" I was dragon-fierce.

"No way. I'm not letting you go alone."

"Then I guess you're coming with me."

Bobby Gene wrinkled his mouth. He'd backed himself into a corner.

Finally he nodded. "We made a deal. If you insist on holding up our end of it, then I'll stand by you." He glared at me. "But no more crazy stunts. No stealing. Nothing dangerous."

"Sure. Yeah, sure." I decided not to remind him that riding a moped might be considered a daredevil stunt by some. Like Mom and Dad.

But we could cross that bridge when we came to it.

# CHAPTER 35

## THINGS AMONG MEN

The next day, Bobby Gene was acting under protest. He refused to pull his weight in the chores. That left me pulling double duty, which was fair under the circumstances.

We cleared brush from the edge of the woods. Cory and I dragged the long branches across the lawn. Bobby Gene skulked behind us. He stood with arms crossed as we snapped them apart to refill the tinderbox.

"What gives?" Cory finally asked.

"I owe him."

"What'd you do?"

I shrugged. "You can stay for lunch. Maybe hang out with Susie after."

"Sounds good." Cory grinned.

We couldn't leave with Styx while Cory was at the house. That would look suspicious. Or in Mom-speak, impolite.

We hung around after lunch, long enough for Dad to get home. Mom left for her shift at the hospital.

Styx rapped on the screen-door frame. He cupped his face against the mesh and looked in. "You guys coming out, or what?"

I swallowed the first words that came to my mouth. *What did you get us into?*

It wasn't okay. There were things we needed to talk about. It was gonna be hard. It was gonna get real.

Styx knew it. "We good?" He shuffled his feet. "Or you bailing?"

"Cory's still here. Want to come in?"

Styx flicked his thumb across his lips. "Uh, yeah," he said.

"Perfect," Dad declared, the moment Styx walked across the threshold. "Why don't we toss it around a bit?" He went out into the garage and returned with one of about every kind of ball we owned. He looked excited.

Cory and I sat on the porch steps with Susie. Dad, Bobby Gene, and Styx tossed the football around.

"Bobby Gene here's got a good frame on him," Dad bragged. "Teaching him some defense, some blocks."

"Right on," Styx agreed.

"Caleb's my idea man. More of a coach than a player. Right, buddy?"

"I guess."

We all knew I wasn't very sporty, but we didn't usually say it out loud. I'd make a terrible coach, to boot. Usually, coaches had to care a lick about the game and know its rules. I wasn't good at any of the things that were important to Dad. Did he have to rub that in? In front of Styx?

Dad was talking more than I'd ever heard before. How did Styx manage it? I listened real close, wanting to be in on the conversation.

Cory kept chatting me up, though. "... a cousin is almost as good as a sibling, right?"

"Better." My eyes were on Bobby Gene, in the thick of things with Dad and Styx. He was terrible at the game, but it looked like he was having fun. "Cousins are better, because you don't have to take them home with you."

Cory sighed. "How come you act like it's wrong to like babies?"

"Not wrong. Just . . ." I grinned, trying to picture his big, bad uncle dude snuggling an infant. "Is she going to wear diapers with 'Harley-Davidson' on them?"

"They sell onesies," Cory retorted.

I cracked up. "What?"

Cory chuckled. "Uncle Greg has all the HD swag you can imagine. Including a pack of onesies and a tiny leather jacket."

"I'm gonna need to see a picture of that."

"Sure thing," Cory said. "I'll take lots of pictures. Uncle

Greg says all's I gotta do is mow his lawn once a week, and I can hang out with the baby as much as I want."

"That's neat." Susie sat on Cory's lap and I let her grip my finger and suck on it.

When Cory finally left, Dad said, "We're evens now. How about a little two-on-two?" He looked at me eagerly. I slid down the porch stairs and scooped up the basketball lying at my feet. Great. What would Styx think when he saw how often I missed the hoop?

We had business to attend to, but Dad and Styx were smiling like nothing I'd seen in a while. I had no choice.

We played until dinnertime. Dad and Bobby Gene versus Styx and me. Those teams made things almost fair. Every time I made a basket, Styx pounded my fist. Every time I missed, he said, "Shake it off; we still got 'em." I had never hated basketball less.

No one even hinted that we should try to get away. Dad smiled a lot. It was like he forgot all my faults for a while.

Dad made chicken shish kebabs for dinner on the grill. The red peppers and onions on the skewer were slathered in so much sauce, you could hardly blame them for being healthy.

"A dinner among men," Dad proclaimed.

I sat a little taller. Men. We cheered with our chicken kebabs.

Susie giggled and Dad kissed her slobbery cheeks. "No, I

didn't forget you." He handed her a small bite of prechewed chicken.

We still had marshmallows left over from the campfire. We toasted them over the grill and sat on the porch as the sun went down. Now that Styx had a taste for s'mores, he couldn't let up. We ate until we were stuffed. Then we laughed our way through the sugar high.

A surprisingly perfect day.

So why did I feel worse than ever underneath?

# CHAPTER 36

## PIKE'S PLACE AUTO PARTS

Bobby Gene sat on the floor of our bedroom with the cordless phone and the actual paper phone book. I walked in after breakfast and found him paging through it.

"What are you doing?"

"We saw the name on the garage," he said. "Pike's Place Auto Parts. We can call them and see if we can find out who Styx made the deal with."

I plopped down next to him. "That's good. Once we sort this out, we can keep doing what we need to with Styx."

Bobby Gene nodded. But I could tell he didn't really believe.

Actually, though, it was perfect. We'd set our minds at ease and the Grasshopper would be ours, free and clear. No guilt. Yesterday with Dad had proved that following Styx could fix everything.

Bobby Gene dialed. He held the phone tipped away from his ear so we could both listen.

"Pike's Place, Marcus Pike speaking."

The gruff old voice caused Bobby Gene's eyes to bug out a bit. "Uh—Mr. Pike?" he said. "Hello. This is—"

I smacked him. "Don't tell him our names," I whispered.

"Hello?" Marcus Pike said. "Who's there?"

Silence.

"Mr. Pike," I said. "We were wondering . . . that is . . . we have a question about an engine situation. We—"

"Who is this?" the gruff voice snapped. "Are you the boys that stole from my lot?"

Bobby Gene slammed the phone down, punching it off with his thumb. We stared at it for a long moment.

"Why'd you do that?" I asked.

"Now we know for sure."

But we didn't.

All I knew for sure was that Styx Malone knew how to fix everything. Styx deserved our trust.

✦ ✦ ✦

It was the worst fight we'd ever had.

Mom interrupted us three (count them: *three*!) times for yelling. It was some kind of miracle that she didn't pick up on what we were fighting about. We tried extra hard to keep our voices down.

"Styx must've had a reason for not telling us everything."

"We did something bad, Caleb. It's not okay."

"We haven't even given him a chance to explain. Maybe it's okay. You don't know."

"Didn't you hear Mr. Pike on the phone?"

"We can't walk away," I said.

"Stolen goods! We could go to prison!"

"They don't send kids to prison."

"They send black kids to prison."

I swallowed hard after that one. All Dad's reminders echoed. *No sudden movements. Keep your hands where they can see them.*

My hands shook.

We stole. We stole. But maybe we didn't. Maybe we were wrong.

"The fireworks were stolen," I reminded him. "How come that was okay?"

"We didn't steal them."

I glared at him. "That's loose."

"We didn't know for sure! This time, we do."

I tried a different tack. "We have a deal with Styx."

"So? It doesn't include lying."

"Dad always says you should see things through even when it doesn't go how you thought," I insisted.

"That's not true when you're breaking the law. Even Dad would say so."

He was right. He was right. I knew he was right. And yet, I flashed on yesterday. Us and Styx and Dad, with laughter and s'mores and even basketball.

"I don't care!" I shouted. "He's our only chance."

I knew that too, as sure as the carpet beneath my feet.

"What are you talking about?" Bobby Gene said.

"You don't care if you're special or not," I said. "You wouldn't understand."

"Everyone's special, in their own way," Bobby Gene said. It was something Mom liked to say.

"Styx is different."

The worst part was, I didn't care that we had stolen. The part of me that was upset about that was matchbox-small compared to the part of me that wanted everything Styx had promised us.

There was something truer than the truth.

There was something more honest about the lies.

Styx understood something no one else did. If bending the rules was the only way to be free, to be happy, to be un-ordinary . . . then I had to do it. I had to.

I climbed the ladder to my bunk and tossed myself over the railing. My comforter bunched up around me. I kicked it aside until it was just me against the bare sheet. It didn't feel any better.

Bobby Gene's huffy breathing ascended. "Caleb."

"Go away." He couldn't understand. He would never understand. His brow furrowed at me. He looked exactly like Dad.

I rolled to face the wall.

"If it means that much to you, I'm . . . not going to stand in your way," Bobby Gene said. "I only hope you know what you're doing."

# CHAPTER 37

## LINCHPIN

I knew exactly what I was doing, thank you very much. In the morning I marched down to Styx's office, with Bobby Gene trailing me.

"We called Pike's Place," I announced. "Why did you lie to us?"

Styx half-smiled. "You're checking up on me?"

"Protecting our investment," I said.

"That's diligent. You make good associates." He flicked invisible ash off his candy cigarette.

"Don't think you can get out of anything by complimenting us," I said.

"What did Pike say?" Styx asked. "What'd you tell him?"

Bobby Gene and I glanced at each other. I described the exchange.

"So, you didn't stay on the line? You didn't even talk

it out with him?" Styx shook his head. "And there you go thinking the worst of me right off. Some friends you are."

"But—but . . . ," Bobby Gene sputtered.

"Mr. Pike's never gonna miss that old motor. Trust me." Styx puffed the candy cigarette. It didn't take much effort to imagine a cloud of smoke wafting from his lips. My hand almost moved to wave it away.

"How can we trust you?" Bobby Gene demanded. "You lied."

"You made thieves out of us!" I cried. "We're accessories to Grand Theft Motor."

Styx laughed. "A rash of GTM breaks out across the Midwest." He arced his hand through the air like a banner headline.

"This is serious."

"He owed me, okay? Don't even worry about it."

"We are worried about it," Bobby Gene said. "We don't want to go to jail."

"I wouldn't let you guys get in that kinda trouble," Styx assured us. "Look, if you told Pike it was all for me, he'd have been fine about it."

"He didn't look fine when he was chasing after us."

"We traded him the lunch box. In your big investigation, did you even ask him if he liked it?"

We hadn't.

Styx waved his hand at us. "Forget this. I shoulda known

you weren't up for it. Just a couple country boys, right? You like everything straight and simple."

That stung.

"Forget you." Styx shoved away from the tree and started back toward his house. We plunged after him.

"Why are you following me?" Styx demanded.

"You owe us an explanation."

"Why? Obviously you believe what you want to. I don't need you."

Bobby Gene was indignant. "You don't get to just walk away!" he shouted. "We *stole* with you. And we didn't tell on you or anything. 'Cause that's what friends do."

Silence.

Finally Styx said, "You're still here."

True.

I swallowed hard. "Yeah, so what of it?"

"So, you're mad. You hate me now, like everyone else. Why don't you just go?"

"We don't hate you," Bobby Gene piped up. "We're disappointed." Whoa, he sounded like Mom and Dad. I would've laughed out loud if it hadn't all been so serious.

"Whatever." Styx bit down too hard on his candy cigarette. It snapped in half. He spat away the piece in his mouth and kept puffing on the part in his hand.

"Bottom line is, you don't want to play anymore, right? That's what you're saying?"

"Of course we do."

"You do?" Styx's eyes brightened. Then he chilled himself out, raising a shoulder. "You do, huh?"

"Just don't lie to us."

"I didn't l—" Styx paused. Sighed. "Mr. Pike is an old . . . friend, okay?"

"How are you friends with a guy like that?" I asked.

Styx walked himself in a little circle, shaking his head. "I used to live at his place. For a little while."

My eyes narrowed. I followed a hunch. "How little a while, Styx?"

Styx steamed in a circle around us. "Kind of a while, okay? I don't want to talk about it."

"Why'd you leave?" Bobby Gene asked.

"Same as always," Styx said. His eyes flashed defiantly. "He didn't want me anymore."

Who wouldn't want Styx? Mr. Pike must be a mean old man with no imagination.

"Well, he's obviously dumb," I blurted out.

"He's not," Styx rushed to say. "He's just real set in his ways. He collects those stupid lunch boxes." He shrugged. "I actually thought he'd like it."

"We need to make it right with him," Bobby Gene said.

Styx hesitated like maybe he was going to argue. But then he said, "Yeah, all right. Lemme think about it."

"No, that's the only deal," Bobby Gene said.

Styx nodded. "I mean, lemme think how to go about it."

Bobby Gene stuck out his hand and they shook on it.

Styx puffed on the stub of his candy cigarette. "Caleb and B. G. Franklin, huh?" He squinted at us through the make-believe smoke. "I guess I underestimated you."

"Damn straight," I said. Those words didn't sound right coming out of my mouth. "I mean, darn tootin'!" I chucked my fist up, real intrepid-like.

"Ouch." Styx smacked his forehead, then clutched his chest. "That actually hurt me in my heart. Y'all so country. Man, do we have some work to do."

We laughed together that time.

"Don't give up on us yet," I told him. "I might have found our missing link."

Styx tossed aside his cigarette stub. "Oh, yeah? Tell us."

"Better to show you." I held up my hand. "Let me take the lead on this one."

They followed me out of the woods. "And bring that motor," I called over my shoulder. "We're gonna need it."

✦ ✦ ✦

We headed over to Cory Cormier's place. Styx didn't have a bike, so we walked ours.

"Tell Styx and B.G. what you told me yesterday," I said. "About your deal with your uncle."

Cory shrugged. "All's I gotta do is mow his lawn once a week and I can hang out with the baby as much as I want."

Styx's whole being zoom-focused on Cory. "So, your uncle has a push mower?"

"Naw," Cory said. "That's why I've gotta do it with ours."

"He doesn't have a mower at all?" Styx glanced at me. We'd hit the escalator-trade lottery.

I pushed in front of Styx. I had this. "Cory, Cory." I tossed my arm around his shoulders. It didn't quite work, on account of him being taller than me. "Your uncle's taking advantage of you."

He looked confused. If only I had a candy cigarette.

"We can help you."

"Help me how?"

"Your uncle's got you doing two chores—babysitting and lawn mowing—and he's got you thinking it's a good deal," I said. "Why don't we all walk over there and offer him an even better deal."

"Like what?" Cory said. "I want to play with the baby."

Cory might have been tough as a Harley fender, but he was just about as bright.

I squeezed his back, real confident-like. My other arm arced in front of us, the way I'd seen Styx do. Painting a picture. "We offer him your babysitting services, plus the riding lawn mower of his dreams."

"In exchange for what?" Styx said.

This was the brilliant part. Styx-level brilliant, if I did say so myself. "Five hundred bucks' worth of Harley-Davidson swag."

# CHAPTER 38

## MEMORABILIA

Cory followed us to the crossroads where our mower was still parked. Bobby Gene and Cory rode their bikes and I balanced on my own handlebars in front of Styx. It didn't take very long at all on wheels.

"I don't understand," Cory said. "Why do you want to give Uncle Greg a riding mower?"

Styx tinkered with the engine, setting the new motor in place.

"He needs one, doesn't he?" I said.

"I guess."

"We're in the business of helping people this summer. Just like we helped you with those fireworks." Risky to mention the fireworks, but I took a chance.

Cory nodded. "That was all right, I guess."

"So now we've gotta unload this beast." I patted the tire. "And who better to help than your uncle?"

Styx closed the mower's hood. "Should be ready."

It had taken him no time at all. I wondered how long he'd lived with Mr. Pike. And how many engines they'd worked on together.

Styx hopped up into the driver's seat. The mower grunted and coughed to life. Styx whooped and lightly slapped the steering wheel. "That's what I'm talking about!"

We cheered.

Styx steered the mower onto the road. We ran for our bikes.

"Lead the way to Uncle Greg's," I told Cory. "Think how happy he'll be to see this baby roll up."

Cory grinned and pedaled ahead of us. "Do you s'pose he'll still let me mow?" he called. "I wanna drive that thing."

"Maybe," I said. "But I wouldn't mention that until after the trade is done."

The mower's top speed was pretty slow. Styx popped in his earbuds and rode patiently, bopping and singing from on high. The rest of us biked in circles around him as he motored steadily up the road.

We pulled into Uncle Greg's driveway. Cory was first off his bike and up the porch. "Uncle Greg?" he yelled through the screen.

"If this works, it'll be a miracle," Bobby Gene said.

"No such thing as miracles," Styx answered immediately. He climbed down from the mower. "Can't count on nothing but your own smarts. Can't count on nobody but yourself."

"You're wrong," Bobby Gene said softly.

Styx pretended not to hear.

"Hey, Uncle Greg," Cory was saying.

"Whatcha doing here, squirt?" The large man filled the doorframe, and then some.

"Boy, have we got a deal for you!" Cory spoke so earnestly it was hard not to laugh.

Styx stepped forward. "We heard you are in the market for lawn mowing services, and we thought we'd do you one better. We propose a trade."

We explained the plan.

"Congrats on the baby, too," I said. "Cory thought this would be exactly what you need right now."

Uncle Greg scratched his stubbled neck. He eyed the lawn mower. "Yeah, couldn't hurt."

"Pretty big lawn," Styx said. "This'll get it done in a jiffy."

"I'm just supposed to trust some kids who show up with a lawn mower?"

"They're my friends," Cory said. "Anyway, my babysitting services are still part of the deal. I can't wait."

"It's in good shape," Styx assured him. "And we can get you parts and labor at a deal. But you won't need that for a while."

"What do you want with my Harley memorabilia?"

I made note of that word. *Memorabilia*. By comparison, *swag* sounded cheap.

"We're in the business of helping people out." Styx neatly sidestepped the question. And he copied my very own words to do it. "We'll take good care of your things."

"Memora . . . bilia is very important to us," I added. "Cory tells us you have an impressive collection. Can we see it?"

When in doubt, flatter. Uncle Greg pushed open the screen door and let us inside.

Twenty minutes later, we walked out. We were lighter by one riding lawn mower, and hauling two bags of Harley-Davidson sw—memorabilia.

✦ ✦ ✦

We had to walk our bikes home, balancing a bag on each seat as we went. Styx pushed my bike, Bobby Gene pushed his, and I walked in between them, hands out to steady the stuff.

Cory peeled off toward his own neighborhood. "See you tomorrow."

"Looking forward to it." I smiled as big as I could. "Thanks for your help today. You ended up with the best deal of all. Just think of all the riding and baby snuggling you'll get."

Cory grinned. "You guys are the best." He rode off, no further questions asked.

I was on fire. A powerful grin and a lotta smooth talk—did Styx Malone feel like he was looking in a mirror?

"We can't leave these things outside overnight," Styx said. "They'll get all dewy."

"Should we each take a bag?" Bobby Gene suggested.

Styx half-smiled. "Equal risk, equal rewards?"

"As usual." We smiled too.

But Styx shook his head. "It's better if you keep them. I can't come into my house with valuable goods like these."

The way he said it made me sad. "Why not?"

Styx's shoulder popped up. "Oh, you know."

But I didn't. All I knew was not to ask again. We had still never been to Styx's house, not really. Only to pick him up.

"Is it bad for you, at home?" I said, braver than usual.

"Nah," Styx said. "It's a decent place. They're nice enough."

"That's good," Bobby Gene said.

"I just can't get too comfortable, right? You never know."

"Never know what?"

Styx pulled a candy cigarette from his pocket, one-handed. "Everything I own fits in a single bag. You never know when you're gonna have to jam."

"Oh."

Of course, we couldn't very well walk into our own

house with the stuff either. We ended up stationing Styx in the flowerbed outside our bedroom. He pushed the bags in through the window.

He smiled at us. "Don't go dipping into the stash without me."

I patted the memorabilia bags. "We'll take good care of them."

"Hey," Styx added as we struggled to replace the screen. "Tomorrow, we get ourselves a Grasshopper."

# CHAPTER 39

## A STRANGER KNOCKS

*Knock, knock.*

Bobby Gene and I scrambled away from the breakfast table, practically tripping over each other to make it down the hallway first. A knock at the door was both exciting and boring, depending on how you looked at it: The knock always held a mystery. But nine times out of ten it was just some grown-up who wanted to talk to Mom or Dad.

Still, we raced for it. My fingers closed around the doorknob first.

"Ha!" I tugged the door open. "Hi," I said to the man on the porch. "How can I—"

Bobby Gene's fingers dug into my arm. We froze, slack-jawed.

Standing on our front porch was none other than Mr. Marcus Pike, of Pike's Place Auto Parts.

"Ayup," he said. "Looks like I've come to the right house."

Bobby Gene pushed me behind him. His chest puffed up. "How did you find us?"

The older man shifted his hat from one hand to the other. "Caller ID."

I smacked Bobby Gene's hand off me. "See, I knew calling was a bad idea."

"Is your father home? Or your mama?"

"They're home," I said. "But your business is with us."

"Heh," he chuckled. "Not how we do things."

"We have money to pay for the engine," Bobby Gene blurted. "We didn't mean to steal anything. We're not like that."

I elbowed him to stop his babbling. "We traded you a lunch box."

"Who is it, Caleb?" Dad's voice preceded his footsteps down the hallway.

Mr. Pike raised a hand. "Mr. Franklin, sir?"

"Yes?" Dad had on his wary voice. "What are you selling?"

"Not a thing," the man says. "Just hoping for a little conversation. It's regarding your boys here. And some of my property."

"No, Dad." I turned around, trying to push him back. "We can handle this."

"What's going on?" Dad pushed the screen door open.

"Could be a misunderstanding," Mr. Pike said.

They spoke over our heads like we weren't even there.

"You mind stepping out to talk with me in private for a minute? I won't take up much of your time."

Dad looked at the man, then at the old truck in the driveway. It had PIKE'S PLACE AUTO PARTS stenciled on the door. Some kind of look passed between them. Working man to working man.

Dad stepped back, keeping his arm extended to hold the screen open. "Come in."

Marcus Pike shuffled down the hallway after Dad.

"Boys, go to your room."

"But he's here because—it's to do with us," I said. "We can explain."

"Go to your room," Dad repeated. "And shut the door."

Our house was not very big, but it was hard to eavesdrop from behind a closed door. Bobby Gene lay on his bed and covered his eyes. I pressed my ear to the seam around the hinges. All I could hear were muffled voices.

✦ ✦ ✦

Mr. Pike stayed half an hour. By the time he left my ears were raw from pressing against the door, and I still hadn't heard much. No doubt we were being accused of stealing. We sorted out our story and got ourselves ready to testify on our own behalf.

When we heard footsteps in the hall, we scrambled away from the door.

Mom barged in without knocking. She found us sitting side by side on Bobby Gene's bed. Heads bowed.

"Living room."

We marched toward our trial.

Dad paced in front of the television, which was off. "I don't know where to begin."

We plopped ourselves on the couch. "See, Dad—" I started.

He cut me off. "Mr. Pike lives all the way in Melville. I told him he must be mistaken about seeing you in his yard the other day."

Bobby Gene gulped.

Dad paused and zoomed in on us. "How did you get there? You didn't ride your bikes for thirty miles and back."

Bobby Gene started to shake.

"Answer me!"

"We, um, we hopped a freight train," I said.

Dad glared at me. "This is no time for jokes, Caleb."

Bobby Gene and I glanced at each other. Talk about a no-win situation.

"Does this Styx Malone have a car? Have you been joy-riding around with some reckless teenager? Do you have any idea what could happen?" Dad yelled.

Tears rolled down Bobby Gene's cheeks. He shivered and held his arms close, as if winter had come suddenly. Dad's anger was like a spear to our bellies.

"Nothing happened," I said, my voice rising to match Dad's.

"You could have been pulled over!" Dad thundered at us. "You could have—" He choked on his own words.

Bobby Gene's cries became audible.

"We weren't in a car," I protested.

"Caleb, for the last time . . ."

Dad was never going to believe what we had done. And it might not help our case anyway.

Dad's face was turning purple. "How many times do I have to tell you? We do not leave Sutton. We're safe here. People know us."

I bolted off the couch. "What if we don't want to stay in this stupid, boring town?"

"We have rules in this family for a reason—"

"I don't care!"

"—and you will follow them whether you like it or not."

Mom stood up. "Enough!"

We all froze.

Mom turned to Dad. "Bobby, please go to our room and wait for me." Then she rounded on us. We stared up at her, shell-shocked and speechless. "You both know the rules of this house. There is no excuse for this behavior."

"Sorry, Mom," Bobby Gene mumbled. I couldn't join in. I wasn't sorry.

Mom's gaze lingered on me, taking in my silence. "Very well," she said. "It's done."

What was done? I wondered. We weren't.

First, Mom called Cory Cormier's house and told his mom we weren't coming for chores today. We were grounded.

Then she officially forbade us to hang out with Styx.

# CHAPTER 40

## SHARP

We saw Styx coming through the yard. He didn't know the trouble he was walking into. We snuck out to the porch to warn him before Mom could stop us.

"Hey, Styx."

"What gives?" He sounded miffed. "I thought we had plans."

It was hard to get the words out. "Sorry. Mom says we can't hang out today."

"Oh. Tomorrow?"

Silence.

"We're kind of . . . forbidden."

Styx's brow furrowed. "They found out about the Grasshopper plan?"

I looked over my shoulder, hoping they wouldn't hear. "No, it's . . . Mr. Pike was here. He talked to Dad."

"It's you." Leave it to Bobby Gene to take the direct approach. "We're not allowed to see you anymore."

Styx took a step back. "What?" He was taken aback, which was a thing I had heard people say that had never made sense until this moment.

There was a lot to explain. Bobby Gene and I tripped over each other, trying to get the right words out. The back door opened. Mom said, "Boys, come inside. Styx needs to go home now."

"Forget them. Do what you want," Styx said.

He didn't understand. Everything was different now. We couldn't disobey Mom to her face.

"We can't," Bobby Gene said.

"After everything we've been through, you're just gonna leave me out to dry?" Styx shook his head. "Wow. And to think, for a second there, I really thought—"

"Look, they'll forget," I said.

"Everything will be back to normal in a few days," Bobby Gene agreed.

Styx stuck out his lips. "A few days. I'm supposed to just sit around and wait for *a few days*? I've got better things to do."

He spun away, fumbling in his pocket for the pack of candy cigarettes. Like a lightning bolt, it hit me. The cigarettes actually made him feel better.

"Styx, wait." We scrambled off the porch after him.

Mom's shadow loomed up against the screen door. "Caleb and Bobby Gene Franklin, get your backsides in here right this minute!"

Bobby Gene stopped. I kept running. "Styx, wait."

"Caleb!" Mom shouted. Then she called for Dad. "Bobby, get out here. Caleb!"

Styx looked over his shoulder. He did a double take at the sight of me chasing him. He stopped. Turned. Waited.

"Don't go," I said. "I'm sorry. We're sorry."

"I get it," he said. "You gotta do your family thing." He spat the words at me. "Isn't that so nice."

"Caleb!" Dad thundered. He came running across the yard to get me.

Styx dropped his voice. "Yo, don't dig yourself in deeper on account of me. I can take care of myself."

Dad was there then. Grasping my wrist and tugging me home. "What's the matter with you? You come when your mother calls you, you hear?"

I tried to pull away, but he had me caught. "Styx!" I shouted. "Styx!"

Styx stalked toward the woods, madder than a hornet and all alone.

✦ ✦ ✦

226

Mom and Dad put us on full lockdown. For the rest of the night, we were confined to our room. We were to sit there quietly and think about what we'd done.

The bags of Harley-Davidson memorabilia were stuffed in our closet behind a pile of board games. Maybe destined to rot there forever.

Mom served us dinner on a tray. She didn't say a word.

Soon there would be another big talking-to. We waited. In their silence, we imagined all sorts of horrors. How much did they know about the motor? Did they know we weren't lying about the train?

We lay on the carpet with the Grasshopper model between us. There had to be a way for us to fix things. We couldn't leave Styx hanging out to dry.

"It's our fault as much as his. We knew it wasn't all aboveboard," Bobby Gene said. "You don't have to admit it to anyone else, but you have to admit it to me. You knew, just like I did."

"He made it fun. I didn't care. He made me feel special."

The worst thought right then was how bad Styx must be feeling. I would never forget the look in his eyes when Bobby Gene blurted out, "It's you."

Styx took it like a spear. To the belly, or maybe the heart.

He wasn't entirely magic. He wasn't invincible. He cared.

"First thing tomorrow, we have to go make it up to him."

Bobby Gene shook his head. "Mom canceled chores with Cory."

"Just for today, I think."

"You think they'll let us out tomorrow?"

"To do chores?" I snorted. "They'll *make* us go."

Bobby Gene stared for a while at our bedroom window. I wondered if he was thinking what I'd been thinking. Why wait until morning? We could go see Styx right now. Walking across the woods at night wouldn't be easy, but we could totally do it. We knew the path as well as anything.

Mom stuck her head through the door right then. Further evidence of her ability to read minds.

"Lights out for the night, boys."

✦ ✦ ✦

In the morning, sure enough, chores were on. "You are to go to the Cormiers' house for one hour and then return," Mom said. "Got it?"

"Yes, Mom." We lied through our teeth. We rode our bikes as if to head over to Cory's place, but instead we doubled back to make up with Styx. Spycraft 101.

"Cory will know something's wrong," Bobby Gene said. "He might not cover for us this time."

"It doesn't matter," I answered. "We have to get to Styx."

I had a bad feeling in my stomach. The expression on his face when he'd said *Don't dig yourself in deeper on account of me.* Like he wasn't worth the trouble or something. He had to know he was. And we might be the only people on earth who could tell him.

✦ ✦ ✦

We rode into Styx's yard. He was sitting out on the porch steps, conveniently enough. He was rearranging the straps on the backpack at his feet. And, of course, he was smoking a candy cigarette.

"What are you doing here?" he asked.

We leaned our bikes against the porch, unclipped our helmets and hung them from the handlebars.

"We came to make sure you're all right," I said.

Styx smiled, but it looked fake. "I'm fine. Don't even worry about it."

We came and sat next to him on the steps. "Friends worry," I said. "We didn't mean to hurt your feelings."

Bobby Gene nodded. "Yeah, you know that, right?"

Styx shrugged. "We're good."

"We need to rethink our Grasshopper plan," I said.

Styx rolled his shoulders and tossed us a million-dollar smile. It came out of nowhere, like the sun from behind a raincloud. "Today's the day, gents. Usual time?"

"We're still sort of grounded," Bobby Gene said. "We can't run off."

"Says who?" Styx said. His voice turned supersweet. "Mommy and Daddy?"

Bobby Gene and I looked at each other. "Um, yeah."

He was making fun of us, and it gave me an unfriendly feeling.

"Oh, please." Styx's voice was fierce. "What are they gonna do, kill you?"

We nodded. "Basically."

"But not really, though." Styx's eyes glowed. "Really they're just gonna love you and always be there?"

Bobby Gene frowned. My heart sped up. I could see what Styx was saying. What trouble could we even really get in? The Grasshopper was worth a little bit of grounding. Time with Styx was worth it too.

Styx puffed his candy cigarette. "I want my half of the goods. You owe me that much."

"What are you talking about?" I said.

Styx stood up. "Before you bail on me, I want my payday."

"We're not bailing."

He shrugged both shoulders. "I thought you were all in. Doesn't seem like it anymore."

"We are," I insisted. "This is just a setback. We're still going to get the Grasshopper."

"When? Tomorrow?" Styx asked. "Or the day after, the

day after, the day after?" He pulled the backpack up onto his shoulders.

"Today!" I declared. "Right now."

"We have chores," Bobby Gene reminded me. "And then we have to be home in less than an hour."

I glared at him. I was starting to think he lived to take the wind out of my sails. Just like Dad.

I held out my hand to Styx. "Gimme one of those things," I said. Styx's eyebrow went up. He reached into his pocket and handed me the whole pack.

My fingers shook. I pulled the long, slim candy out of the box. Imagined its tip glowing with all the fire of my heart. I put it to my lips.

Then I looked Styx Malone right in the eye. "Be outside our window at one p.m. sharp."

# CHAPTER 41

## OPERATION: GRASSHOPPER

"Is this going to be difficult?" Bobby Gene asked. We lingered outside the windows of the hardware store, contemplating.

"Don't worry," Styx said. "We got this."

We were outlaws. We'd locked our door and snuck out our bedroom window with the memorabilia bags. We'd lugged them downtown. And now we stood here, fake-smoking like the baddest of the baddies.

Styx threw down the stub of his candy cigarette and ground it out like it was real. It crunched lightly into the sidewalk as he twisted the toe of his boot over it.

"We've been waiting long enough. Let's do this thing."

The jingle of the door chimes never sounded so good. Walking into the shop with the goods to strike a deal made all the difference.

We strolled up to the moped, same as we'd done before.

Lingered until the store clerk wandered over. "You've got a buying face on," he said.

"Yes, sir," Styx agreed. "We'd like to see Mr. Davis."

"I'll call him." The man dialed, spoke shortly and hung up. "Are you sixteen? Got a license?"

"Sure," Styx said. He pulled out his thin wallet and started to show the guy a card.

"We've been eyeing that bike through the window for a month," Styx added. "We came in ready to buy it, but I've got some questions now. The back looks smaller than I thought. How big's the gas tank?"

"Oh, it's a full two gallons." The salesman barely glanced at Styx's ID. "Bigger than it looks, for sure."

"Two gallons? In that little space?" Styx sounded disappointed. "There must not be much room left for carrying stuff. I don't know about that."

The clerk scooted around the counter to talk us up about the bike. "Let's take a look," he said. "I'll show you."

He circled his hands over the bike, like a magician about to pull out a rabbit; then he popped open the seat to show us the cargo pocket. For the next few minutes he ran us all over that bike from top to bottom. We knew all this, but Styx was working his magic.

Bobby Gene's eyes grew bigger, taking in the flames on the thorax and the bright green of the whole Grasshopper. It was hard not to stare. Our victory was so close.

Styx did himself proud through the sales pitch. We knew how bad he wanted that bike, but you wouldn't have known it to look at him.

Mr. Davis walked in. "Ah, you're back. Here to make me an offer?"

"Sure thing." Styx shook the owner's hand. Bobby Gene and I started pulling out the memorabilia.

"What's all this?" Mr. Davis was not impressed.

"It's your perfect trade, like we promised," I said.

We laid the pieces out one by one. A pair of shades, like Cory's. A roadside repair kit. A leather vest. A wall clock. A car license plate holder that said MY OTHER CAR'S A HARLEY. A set of four highball glasses. Each with the genuine Harley-Davidson logo prominently placed.

"What do I want with a bunch of Harley stuff?" Mr. Davis grunted. "Perfect trade, my elbow."

"It is, though," Styx said. "Give them to your son. You've got birthdays and Christmases taken care of for a couple of years with all this. It's good stuff any motorcycle enthusiast would love."

Mr. Davis stared at the items. "I don't know."

I moved closer to him and laid my hand on his arm. "I know what you want most," I whispered. I knew, because I felt it, all the way to the bottom of my heart and back. "I'm sorry . . . that you're having a hard time with your son."

Mr. Davis looked at me. His eyes shimmered. "I love that boy. Why can't he see that?"

"Maybe he doesn't know what to do." The words poured out of me. "Doesn't mean he can't see how you feel."

Mr. Davis didn't move.

It wasn't working. My brilliant idea was going to fail. We'd be left with nothing. My hope and excitement started swirling, as if to drain away.

Who was I kidding? I didn't have the skills to pull off this crazy trade. I looked up at Styx, who was watching me work. I waited for him to put on a smile and sweet-talk Mr. Davis in a whole different direction. He could still fix my mistake.

Instead, Styx put his hand on my shoulder. "You see, Mr. Davis? It is perfect. These gifts would show him you support his choices, and he'll see how much you care. How you want to do right by him."

We stood like that for one endless moment. The energy of Styx Malone passed through me, straight into Mr. Davis. Our combined powers, maybe, would be enough.

Finally the owner slapped his thigh and nodded. "Can't hurt to try."

# CHAPTER 42

## MAKING AMENDS

We walked out of the shop with the new moped in hand. Bobby Gene held the door open, Styx rolled it through and I carried the helmets. The Grasshopper came with two. We'd bought the third, even though Styx said, "Nah, I'm good." Mom had drilled bike safety lessons so far into us that we couldn't imagine it any other way.

"That was so amazing," I crowed.

"I can't believe that worked!" Bobby Gene tried on a helmet. Slapped it, laughing.

Styx high-fived each of us. "We make a good team."

We pushed the Grasshopper around the corner to the gas station and filled it up. Paid fireworks cash for our two gallons and bought three bottles of strawberry milk while we were at it. We were feeling flush.

Styx sat straddling the moped as we chugged the drinks.

A major escalator transaction works up a powerful thirst. We tossed the empty bottles away.

"Hop on," Styx said. He scooted forward, clipping on his helmet. The seat was long.

I put on mine, too, and jumped on behind him. Bobby Gene watched.

"We can all fit," Styx said. "Let's take her for a spin."

"Right here on the street?"

Styx laughed. "Where did you think we would ride?"

"I don't know . . . in the country somewhere?"

I slid off the seat. "You go in the middle." Bobby Gene climbed on. The engine hummed to life beneath us.

✦ ✦ ✦

We buzzed along the country roads forever. Every second was exhilarating—better than a bike, better than a car. We were flying through a wind of our own making. Past, present, future, gliding around us.

Finally Styx pulled over at the edge of a soybean field. We could see for miles in all directions. We hopped off and unclipped our helmets.

"That was amazing." My cheeks were windburned. Bobby Gene seemed to have forgotten about us being thieves.

Styx hadn't. He pointed across the field to a pair of buildings.

Bobby Gene recognized it before I did. "Mr. Pike's place."

"You said, to keep hanging, we had to make it right," Styx reminded us. "Best I can think is, we walk up and ask him what else he wants in payment."

Bobby Gene nodded. "Yeah."

"If it's like I say, and it's fine already, then we're settled. If it's like you think, and he's mad, we still got cash to make amends."

"Yes. Brilliant," I said.

We left the moped in the middle of the field. No sense calling attention to it, Styx said. We walked over to Pike's Place.

Knocked.

Nothing.

Styx knocked again. We waited.

"Guess he's not here," Bobby Gene said. "Should we leave a note?" We didn't have any paper.

Styx was a mix of disappointed and relieved. "Just as well, I guess."

"We could try again tomorrow," I suggested. "Another afternoon ride?"

"Or maybe it's a sign," Styx said. "That we're done here."

"Tomorrow," Bobby Gene said.

But Styx gazed wistfully at the small house.

"Hey," he said. "Whatever happens, at least you can look back and remember me for doing at least one thing right. Trying, anyway." He offered a lopsided smile, then struck up a candy cigarette for the walk back to the moped.

"Lots of right things," I said. We trooped along through the soybeans.

Styx, from that day, lives in my mind like a series of snapshots. Styx, by the roadside, straddling the bike, with joy stamped across his face. Styx, gazing across the field, looking nervous and kind of scared. Styx on Pike's porch, thoughtful and still. Hands clutched in his pockets.

I can see it all now.

That day, we had no idea.

+ + +

The second ride was even better than the first. Styx parked the moped in the woods behind his house. "I'm the one who can drive it, for now," he said. "Okay to park it here?"

We nodded. We sure couldn't show the Grasshopper around our house. We started toward his house with him, where we'd left our bikes in the morning.

"Let's go again tomorrow," we said.

Styx's feet got kinda shifty. "Oh, sure. Yeah. Let's play it by ear."

That was weird. We saw each other every day. Why would tomorrow be any different?

"Sure," I said. "I mean, we could go fishing instead, if you wanted." *But that would be crazy,* I wanted to add. We had the Grasshopper!

"Listen, guys," Styx said. "This has been great, you know what I'm saying?"

"Yeah," we agreed. The Grasshopper was everything we'd hoped for. We could go anywhere. Do anything.

Styx reached out and smacked us each on the shoulder. "Whatever happens, just remember: Y'all are cool. And I said so."

"Sure," we said.

Styx fidgeted with the moped handlebars like he wanted to say something more. It was strange. Usually we said "see you later" and took off in our own directions.

"What?" I asked.

"It's nothing," Styx said.

"Okay. See you tomorrow." We waved.

Styx gazed at the Grasshopper. "Now that we've got it, I guess I—I mean, we can take off anytime we want, right?"

"Absolutely. So . . . usual time?"

Styx paused. Then he grinned. "Sure thing."

240

# CHAPTER 43

## DCS

We got about five minutes deep into the woods before we remembered.

"Our bikes are still at Styx's house." Bobby Gene said. "We never brought them home this morning." We were so used to walking home from Styx's that we'd forgotten them twice now. They were still leaning against Styx's porch.

"We should go back for them." Mom would definitely be suspicious if she noticed them missing.

"Yeah, but we should walk them through the woods," Bobby Gene said. "We have to sneak back in through our window, remember?"

I grinned. I'd forgotten all about our great escape.

We doubled back.

Something was going on at Styx's place. There was a lot of yelling coming from inside the house. A gray sedan was parked in the driveway. It had DEPARTMENT OF CHILD SERVICES written on the door.

We rushed up onto the porch just in time to hear Styx shout, "Everybody get off my back!"

A chorus of adult voices followed his through the screen windows.

"Forget all of you. I'm out."

A second later, Styx burst through the door. He raced for the stairs, stumbling over toys on the porch as he went. He flailed his arms like a windmill but stayed on his feet.

"Styx," I said. I wasn't sure he even saw us. He ran straight for the woods with his backpack over his shoulder.

I stumbled off the porch after him.

Bobby Gene took one for the team. He stood fast in his spot as a man and a woman dressed in almost-matching gray suits came out.

"Excuse me," he said as they practically barreled into him. He made himself big, clumsily blocking their path.

Sometimes my brother really came through.

The woman called after Styx. "You're not making this any easier for yourself."

Styx was out of sight beneath the trees in seconds. I chased him. Found him shoving his bag into the moped seat.

"I thought we had trust," Styx said. "You betrayed me."

"What? No . . ." We hadn't.

But there was no way to convince Styx Malone once he'd made his mind up about something.

The low feeling in my gut sank lower. "Styx, wait!"

"What's going on?" I heard Bobby Gene asking the gray suits.

I didn't hear the answer, on account of the moped starting up.

# CHAPTER 44

## TWISTED

Styx got on the bike angry.

That low feeling knotted itself tighter. If we make Mom too mad when she's driving, she always pulls over. Says it isn't safe to drive angry.

"Styx, wait!" I shouted. "Don't go."

But he zoomed off in a cloud of dust, exactly the way it always happens in the movies.

"We've gotta go after him," I told Bobby Gene, running for our dirt bikes.

Bobby Gene ran after me. "What's the point?" he said as we flicked our kickstands. "We'll never catch up."

It was a gut feeling, that we should get on our bikes. Bobby Gene was right, we had no chance of catching Styx. I only knew we had to ride. Now.

✦ ✦ ✦

We caught up to Styx at the corner of Lincoln and Starwood. Unfortunately, we caught him because he was stopped. Stopped, beside a pickup truck with a broken headlight and a dented fender.

The pickup truck was green. Not mint green, like the moped. Dark green, like pine trees at dusk. Like grass in the shadows, or a swatch of tree-house paint. I looked at the truck because I didn't want to look elsewhere.

My bike fell to the side. I was already running. Bobby Gene shouted behind me.

Glass crunched under my feet. Styx made a sound like the world was coming to an end, which it was.

*Twisted.*

The only word that came to mind at the sight of Styx Malone.

*Twisted.*

His legs were caught beneath green metal. The moped. *Twisted.*

His right arm was trapped under him, his left arm flung out to the side. His left shoe rested beside his head. His right shoe was nowhere to be seen.

"Oh, Jesus. Oh, God. Lord, have mercy." A man's shadow loomed over us. "He came out of nowhere. I didn't see him."

*Beep beep beep.* The digital pounding of a cell screen.

"Jesus, God— Yes, I need an ambulance." The man paced and prayed and sirens wailed in the distance.

Styx moved. Just a finger, inching across the ocean of shards.

I took his outstretched hand—the only part of him not covered in blood.

"Hold on, Styx. You're going to be okay." My throat was full of not quite believing it.

"Sure," he says. "It doesn't even hurt." His eyes drifted shut.

I knew from TV that that was bad. Shock, or something. When the worst kind of pain goes away, it means—

"Come on. You can't die," I whispered.

Styx's eye opened. "I won't," he murmured. "I don't have that kind of luck."

# CHAPTER 45

## SHOCK

They wouldn't let us ride in the ambulance. We stood amid the broken glass, shoulder to shoulder, while the EMTs worked on Styx. They tore apart the moped around him, tossing the pieces aside.

Everything was coming apart right in front of us.

One piece landed at my feet. S375-681W. All twisted. The letters and numbers blurred. I picked it up anyway.

Bobby Gene picked something up too. A backpack, now all rumpled and scraped. "It's his stuff," Bobby Gene said. "We'll keep it for him."

The paramedics scooped Styx onto their bright yellow board, sliding him flat, like a pancake. His eyes stayed closed. They covered his mouth with a mask to help him breathe. The door shut behind them and the siren howled away.

✦ ✦ ✦

The garage door was open, with the car in the driveway. Mom was bent into the backseat, probably buckling Susie into place.

"Mom! Mom!" Bobby Gene started shouting. We dropped our bikes on the lawn and rushed up to her, breathless.

"Where have you been?" Mom demanded. Her head was still halfway in the car. "Mrs. Cormier said you didn't show up for chores this morning. And sneaking out the window!" She spun out to face us, her fists on her hips. "I was very clear when I told you—"

"Mom!" Bobby Gene continued. I was too shell-shocked to speak. Still holding a piece of the Grasshopper.

Mom's face paled. Her cheeks slacked and her lips rounded. "No. Caleb, what happened?"

Her hands were on me then. Touching my face. Lifting my shirt. Squeezing my arms and stroking my belly and up to my chest.

"Where are you hurt, honey? Tell me what happened."

"I—" Everything felt confusing. The sky and the driveway and the house and the car and Susie gurgling and Mom's hands pressing me, and my skin stung and I couldn't get the words out.

*Accident.*

*Green.*

*Styx.*

*Twisted.*

"Sweetheart," Mom said. "I can't see where you're bleeding. Talk to me."

I didn't understand. Could she see my heart bleeding?

Bobby Gene found the words first. "Styx got run over by a truck."

"What?" Mom gasped.

"The ambulance came and he's not dead. They said we should meet him at the hospital. Riley."

Mom's whole body shook, but she pulled herself together. "Okay, let's get you out of these clothes."

She nudged my shoulder. "Caleb?" When I didn't move, Mom unclipped my helmet and yanked my T-shirt over my head like I was Susie. Right there in the driveway. But my head was spinning so hard I didn't even care.

The shirt in her hand was covered in blood.

"Please finish buckling her in," Mom told Bobby Gene. "We'll be right back." She herded me inside. Straight into the bathroom.

"What is this?" Mom held up the piece of the Grasshopper. "Is it from the accident?" She tossed it into the tub.

"Did you see him get hit?" she asked.

*No. We came after.*

"Was he riding bikes with you?"

*Moped.*

The moped. I couldn't possibly explain.

"It was scary, I'm sure." Mom wiped me down with a warm cloth. I shivered anyway.

"It's okay, baby." Mom wrapped her arms around me. "It's gonna be okay."

She didn't know. She didn't see.

It wasn't okay.

✦ ✦ ✦

Bobby Gene was the one who kept his cool. We got in the car and he told Mom the whole story. Starting with how we went over to apologize to Styx after lunch (he slid that fib in there smooth) and how we found the DCS people and how Styx was upset. There was no way to avoid mentioning the moped, but Bobby Gene kept calling it a bike, so I supposed Mom could picture it however she wanted.

I stared at my palm, resting on my thigh. The pressure of Styx's hand in mine still hovered there, ghostlike.

"He's dead," I whispered. "Styx is dead."

Bobby Gene frowned. "No, he isn't."

"He looked dead."

"They said he wasn't," Bobby Gene snapped.

"I think they lied." My voice rose higher and higher like a balloon with the string let go. "He's dead!"

"Boys," Mom scolded, in her I'm-worried-don't-mess-with-me voice. We shut up.

"He's going to be okay," Bobby Gene whispered. He stuck his arm across the car seat between us. I gave him my hand. Susie flopped her fat fists against our forearms.

I might have felt better if he'd reached over and smacked me. Like normal.

Worry about Styx was the only thing on my mind. I didn't register what was happening at first. Not as Mom zipped us along the county road. Not even when she whirled us up the ramp to the expressway.

Soon the Indianapolis skyline loomed up in the distance. Small, at first. Like a LEGO city.

That was when the jolt singed my throat. It sizzled my skin.

*No. Not like this.*

Styx had kept his promise. He'd gotten us to Indy.

# CHAPTER 46

## HOSPITAL SMELL

"We need to speak to his parent or guardian," the nurse said calmly. Tile underfoot. White all around.

"I don't have the direct number," Mom said. "I can only tell you where they live."

"He has a driver's license," Bobby Gene said. "It has to have his number on it." We had never called Styx. He was always just there, or else we knew where to look for him.

Mom pushed her arm against Bobby Gene's chest, nudging him back. Closing the circle between her and the nurse. A grown-ups-only zone. *We-are-being-serious-here-step-back.*

"We called the number on his license and left a message." The nurse answered the question from within the circle. "It was some kind of auto repair business."

Outside the circle, things felt pretty serious too. Auto repair. Repair. Repair. My mind orbited around this word. It felt important.

"He's a foster child," Mom said. "He'll be in the DCS system as well. My husband spoke to them about him just yesterday."

My brain snapped to attention. Bobby Gene gasped.

Dad was the one who'd reported Styx?

✦ ✦ ✦

We sat in the waiting room all afternoon, because that's what the loved ones do on TV. And that's what they called them on TV, "loved ones." Even though Styx Malone was convinced he had never been loved.

I laid my head on my arms. The hospital had this smell, you know? A scent that made my nose feel full and my head feel light and achy. It made it hard to breathe. How were you supposed to heal in a place where it was hard to breathe?

Bobby Gene put his hand on my back. "It's okay," he said. "Styx is going to be okay."

"We don't know that." My thick-throated words hung heavy in the air.

"There's no cause for pessimism," Bobby Gene said. I swear, sometimes it was like he'd inhaled Essence of Dad and was breathing it back out. Like the opposite of talking goofy after sucking helium. "Staying positive helps."

"Shut up, B.G.," I snapped.

"Stop calling me that."

I lifted my head to look at him. "What?"

"How come you guys always call me that?"

"You don't like it?" I was stunned.

Bobby Gene shrugged. "Well, I don't mind it that much usually. But right now . . ." He looked toward the scary tall doors of the ER.

"I wish I had a nickname." I fisted the tears off my cheeks.

"You don't need one," Bobby Gene said.

"My name is ordinary."

"*My* name is ordinary," Bobby Gene said. "Everyone we know is named the same as me. It's not like we know any other Calebs. Not even famous ones."

I thought about that.

"Honeys," Mom said. "We need to go home now." Susie fussed in her arms.

"We didn't get to see him," Bobby Gene said.

We needed to see him. In my mind, all I saw was Styx twisted. They could keep telling us he was alive, but it wouldn't feel true until he was right in front of us, joking like usual. I wondered if they would let him have candy cigarettes in the hospital.

Mom gripped Susie tighter, wrestling her out of an attempted swan dive. "You won't get to see him today. We'll come back."

But we wouldn't. I could see it in her eyes.

"We can wait," Bobby Gene said.

Mom shook her head. "We'll come back. I promise."

I sat up straighter. "You promise?"

Mom sighed, looping Susie over her forearm. "Five more minutes," she said. "I'll pull the car around right over there." She pointed to the circle drive under the ER portico, beyond the big sliding glass doors. "When you see me, you come outside, okay?"

Our track record for obedience was not so great this week. We nodded anyway.

# CHAPTER 47

## MIRAGE

"I'm not getting in the car," I said. If the situation was reversed, Styx would stand by us. How could we abandon him?

Bobby Gene shook his head. "Yes, you are."

I glared at him. The gulf between us had been growing all summer. A canyon. Me and Styx on one side, Bobby Gene on the other. With Dad, and everything ordinary.

We sat in silence, waiting to see what would happen. We had one eye on the ER doors and one eye watching for Mom.

Mom took longer than five minutes, which turned out to make all the difference.

✦ ✦ ✦

Mr. Pike rushed in through the sliding doors. He recognized us and came right over.

"Caleb and Bobby Gene," he said. "I get that right?"

"Yes, sir." We stood up and shook his hand.

"How's he doing?" he asked.

"Well, we don't really know much," I said. "They won't let us in."

Mr. Pike looked at the ER doors. "They don't tell ya anything around here, eh?"

"How'd you know?" Bobby Gene asked.

Mr. Pike chuckled. "I been round the block a few times. Not like either one of you." He tapped me gently on the shoulder.

It was interesting. Here, where there was no yelling, no motor, no parents, and no Styx, he seemed . . . kind.

"I tell ya," Mr. Pike said. "I don't know what I'm gonna do with that boy."

"You know him pretty well, huh?" I asked. I guess I'd been wondering it all along.

"He lived with me for three years." Mr. Pike shook his head. "Never could forgive me for letting him go. Wasn't my choice."

"What happened?"

He tilted one shoulder, a tiny hitch that held a whole story. "No rhyme or reason to how the state does its business."

"They took him away from you?" I pictured the man and woman in their somber gray suits. Villains were supposed to be big and covered with blood or spikes or something. At least, villains who could ruin somebody's whole life.

Mr. Pike slapped his hat against his knee. "Ah, well. Sometimes you gotta take your lumps."

That didn't sound too pleasant.

Mr. Pike studied us. "You know, this is the longest he's ever stayed in one place before trying to run away."

"He ran away?" Bobby Gene asked.

Mr. Pike grunted a laugh. "Nine times. They brought him back after the first three. Then I stopped reporting it. He'd come back on his own. Heh. Always showing up, like a bad penny."

"He's not bad," I said.

"Heck, I know that." Mr. Pike slapped his hat against his knee.

"It hurts not to be wanted," Mr. Pike mused. "I tried to show him the kinda care he should get. Heh. But with that one, it's tough love a lot of the time." He eyed us. "You two managed to be good friends to him."

"Yeah, we love him," Bobby Gene said, like it was a foregone conclusion.

We knew, but Styx didn't. The look in his eye when he'd gotten on the moped the last time . . . I couldn't shake that.

I cleared my throat. We had made a deal with Styx, after all. About making things right. "We still owe you a motor, I guess."

"Nah." Mr. Pike smiled sadly. "I'd've given him the dog-gone thing if he woulda knocked on the door and asked."

✦ ✦ ✦

Mr. Pike went to try to get info from the nurse.

Mom pulled up. She stood outside the glass doors, waving at us to come outside.

The moment of truth. Was I going to make my stand?

I planted my feet. I listened to my belly. I was a tree, a rock, a mountain. I would not be moved from this spot until I knew Styx Malone was all right. Not until they let us see him.

Across the room, through the glass, Mom's expression shifted. She was looking at me, and I could tell she knew what was about to happen.

Bobby Gene tapped my shoulder.

"No," I said.

He tapped harder. And pointed. His face said "Look," so I did.

Lo and behold, who should come strolling down the hall?

None other than Styx Malone.

# CHAPTER 48

## EFFECTS

In the cartoons, when you think you're seeing a mirage, you rub your fists into your eyes and it clears right up.

Styx Malone was no mirage.

We leaped up and ran to him.

"Take it easy," he warned.

We didn't. The air oofed out of his lungs as we threw our arms around him.

He groaned. "Stop, I'm all banged up."

I swear, we hugged him harder. We couldn't help it.

"Ow. Guys."

We pulled back. Styx wore a blue-dotted hospital gown and a bandage on his forehead. His right arm was bandaged up with gauze. He walked carefully, pushing an IV pole along with him.

"We thought you were dead!" Bobby Gene's voice was suddenly clogged with tears. "Caleb kept saying you died!"

"Naw. Me?" Styx winked, then grimaced, touching his forehead. "Ow. They gotta send more than a lousy pickup truck to take me down."

I held off my laugh. Styx's expression was too much. He pouted, as if he was disappointed in the universe for not trying harder to get him.

"Mr. Malone, what are you doing out of your bed?" A nurse came storming up. "For heaven's sake. You were in a major accident, young man. You need to be horizontal."

"My bad," Styx said, real easy. "I heard my friends were here, is all."

The nurse glared at us like we were hopelessly germ-riddled. "No visitors in the ER."

Styx winked again as she walked him away. "They call me Mr. Malone around here. I've never been to such a fancy resort."

✦ ✦ ✦

They kept Styx overnight for observation. We rode home as a hungry Susie screamed from her car seat the whole way.

Dad was waiting with pizza when we got home. I picked at a slice of hand-tossed supreme.

I didn't understand why we were getting a pass on all the things we'd screwed up. Dad didn't even ask us to explain. He ate his pizza and nodded while Mom went on about how lucky we were to have a top children's hospital close by. Luck was in the eye of the beholder, I supposed.

*I don't have that kind of luck.* Styx's words ricocheted inside me. I didn't like what he'd said. It didn't even make sense.

Styx being okay mattered more than anything. I knew that. And the day had been so terrible that we weren't even really in trouble anymore. No one was lecturing us about misbehavior or consequences. It was like they just wanted to erase it all and go back to normal.

I couldn't go back.

When Dad got up from the table, he cupped the back of my head and kissed my forehead. Then he went into the family room. The TV snapped on.

I slid away from the table and went to my bed. The Grasshopper model greeted me beside my pillow. A thousand green shards pierced my heart.

"Caleb? Sweetie?" Mom poked her head over the railing.

I rolled toward the wall.

✦ ✦ ✦

That night, we examined Styx's belongings. Until he pulled the stuff out, I'd forgotten that Bobby Gene had rescued the backpack from the moped seat at the scene of the accident. The inventory:

Four packs of candy cigarettes, now reduced to chalky rubble.

Six T-shirts, in various ragged conditions.

A pair of shorts, two pairs of threadbare jeans.

A lump of identical gray boxers.

A toothbrush in a plastic bag. (No paste. No floss.)

A small stuffed frog whose fur had been rubbed dry.

"This is all his stuff," Bobby Gene said. "Why did he have all his stuff with him?"

"This can't be all his stuff," I said. It was so little. "Where's his iPod?"

"He moves a lot, remember?" Bobby Gene reminded me. "He keeps his wallet and iPod in his pocket."

But . . . Styx's words from earlier floated back to me.

*Everything I own fits in a single bag. You never know when you're gonna have to jam. Whatever happens . . .*

*Remember me . . .*

*I—we can take off anytime we want, right?*

My body sank until it met the carpet. My heart kept right on going. "He was leaving us."

# CHAPTER 49

## MIRACLES?

I got up and walked to the bathroom. I wanted to be far from Styx's things, and even farther from their truth.

They say hindsight is 20/20. I know what that means now. When you look back at things, you can see their meaning more clearly, like you have perfect 20/20 vision.

Styx, with the fast feet. Styx, who could almost fly.

Of course he wasn't staying. Of course he wouldn't let himself be stuck in Sutton forever. Like us.

*I can't wait to get out of this town. I can make it on my own, no problem.*

How stupid had I been? Following Styx wasn't our ticket to freedom. The Grasshopper was *his* ticket to freedom. That was what he wanted, right from the beginning.

*I have an idea. Lemme show you. Coolest thing ever . . .*

Did he even care about us at all?

Bobby Gene followed me into the bathroom. We stood

side by side, staring down into the bathtub. The twisted piece of the Grasshopper still lay there. It looked ugly and messy and small.

✦ ✦ ✦

There was nothing pretty about the accident. Nothing neat about the way everything crumpled inside me, seeing him laid out that way, thinking it was all over. No more worries, no more sadness, no more adventures, no more sun.

But he'd survived. The world hadn't seen the last of Styx Malone. No one would stand around and say "He never felt a thing."

Styx felt everything.

So how could he have done this to us?

When I thought back on our summer, I could see it. All the things that echoed with me about him. Freedom. Adventure. Excitement. Did it mean never really caring about anyone?

To be like Styx, to really fly, would I have to leave behind everything?

Bobby Gene knelt beside the tub. He cleaned the shrapnel carefully. I hated him doing it, but I stood there all the same. There was nowhere to go.

Without Styx across the woods, ready to open up the sky, our world had shrunk to this house. This pair of rooms. There was no way out of my own skin.

"Look at this," Bobby Gene said. He pushed the fragment toward me.

No.

I hated the way the metal was twisted, the numbers were all mangled. My eyes blurred. I wanted to grab it and throw it.

"Look what it says." Bobby Gene pointed.

He was holding it upside down. I started to right it, but then I saw what he meant. It said MIRACLES.

✦ ✦ ✦

We looked at the fragment again in the light of day. I was sure it would turn out to be a crazy trick of shadows. But it wasn't. The letters and numbers on the S375-681W were smashed and scratched in such a way that it now looked like MIRACLES.

"Why is it like that?" I said.

Bobby Gene shrugged. "Maybe it's a sign?"

I shook my head. My heart became a cold, hard rock against his words. Styx had been leaving us. And taking the Grasshopper. He'd survived the accident and that was a miracle. But my dream of a bigger world had gotten crushed right along with the moped.

There was nothing miraculous about the storm in my belly.

Cory Cormier rang the front doorbell at ten a.m. He had an odd little bundle of flowers in his hand.

"I picked them from our yard." He shrugged. "Mom says you're supposed to bring flowers when someone's hurt."

"Thanks," we said.

I collected the bouquet from Cory's sweaty fist. "We're not doing chores today," I told him. "We're going back to the hospital."

"Go on and do your chores," Mom said. She pulled down a glass and splashed water in the bottom. The expression on her face gave me a funny feeling. A little motor in my belly revved up.

I stuck the flowers in the water. "We're going back to the hospital," I repeated. It wasn't a question. But it was.

Mom rearranged the stems and fluffed the petals. "Honey . . ."

The angry motor buzzed, full-tilt, inside me. "You promised."

"That was before you saw Styx," she said. "Remember? I promised to bring you back to see him, but then you saw him."

"We have to go again." I narrowed my eyes as my belly revved and rolled. Did she think we couldn't see what she was doing?

Mom sighed. "Your father has the car this morning, anyway. You know that."

I could read between the lines. Mom was willing to take us back. Dad was the one who had said no. Like always.

"But you *promised*!" Bobby Gene crossed his arms and glared. Cory stood awkwardly alongside him.

"I did," Mom acknowledged. "But—I should never have made that promise."

"Did you think we were going to forget?" I said. "You only promised so we'd leave?"

Mom looked pained. "I made a mistake. That happens sometimes."

"We went yesterday!"

"Sweetie, yes. I made a quick decision in an emergency. I—" She paused. "I still think it was the right thing to do. And you saw Styx."

"He's our best friend." And we never told him how special he was. A person needs to hear that sometimes.

"Not today, guys. I'm sorry. Go on and do your chores."

She left the room, like it was the final word.

No way were we doing chores under these conditions. We staged a labor strike.

"I could get used to this," Cory said, flopping onto the patio chaise. We lay there, looking calm, even though I was feeling everything but calm inside.

Mom never said anything about us not working, which

made our strike less dramatic. She opened the back door a while later and announced, "Lunch."

It was a heck of a spread. Cheeseburgers and baked fries, with milkshakes on the side. Guilt food. Delicious guilt food. We were not so noble as to stage a hunger strike.

After lunch, Cory went home. We waited on the front porch until Dad pulled into the driveway. Maybe, just maybe, there was still a chance to get down to see Styx.

"That's a good-looking welcome committee," Dad said. He rubbed Bobby Gene's head. I ducked away. "Why aren't you guys off somewhere?"

"We're upset," Bobby Gene informed him.

Dad should have asked why. He should have sat down with us and explained his stupid rules. But he didn't do any of those things. He rubbed Bobby Gene's head again, glanced at me and went inside.

We waited by the car. Eventually Mom came out, dressed for work. "I'm sorry to disappoint you," she said. "But you know as well as I do that it's not going to happen."

To our credit, we didn't raise a ruckus. Bobby Gene nodded obediently. I looked up at the porch, looked through the screen door at the shadow of Dad standing there.

*Come out and face us,* I wanted to shout. But he didn't.

I turned and walked across the driveway, away.

# CHAPTER 50

## ESCAPE HATCH

I made it all the way to the edge of the Styx woods before I realized I was walking toward nothing.

Bobby Gene followed me.

Everything was ruined. We'd lost the Grasshopper. We'd never be able to visit the city ever again.

Unless.

I turned around and went to the garage. Kicked the stand off my bike and pushed it into the driveway. We'd been to the city now. I'd seen the way to get there. We could go again ourselves. It might take all afternoon, but it would be worth it. To stand by Styx's bedside and be sure he was really all right.

And to say what was on my mind. To scream it at him: *How could you?*

I got on my bike.

"No, Caleb." Bobby Gene put his foot down. I could hear it in his voice.

"I'm going. You don't have to come."

He straddled my front wheel. "No."

"Get out of my way." I would fight him, if I had to. I'd never won in a fight with him, but I'd never had this kind of fire inside me. My sides were made of impenetrable green metal. Flames licked my abdomen, inside and out.

We looked at each other. I knew his face even better than my own. Usually we didn't need a lot of words.

His eyes said things, and mine refused to listen. Between us, a canyon. An ocean.

Finally, my brother sighed and stepped aside.

✦ ✦ ✦

I rode as hard as I could. Didn't look back. Not even when I swore I could hear Bobby Gene's huffy breathing coming down the road after me.

We zoomed down the county road. How long would it take to get to the hospital from here? It didn't matter.

A car coming toward us glinted in the sunlight. It slowed as we passed each other. The plump, light-haired woman behind the wheel glanced out at us. A few beats later, the car U-turned and came rolling up alongside us.

A familiar, grinning voice called to us out the window. "Well, if it isn't Caleb and Bobby Gene Franklin. Fancy meeting the two of you here."

✦ ✦ ✦

We jumped off our bikes and ran right up to the car. The county road was flat enough that we could see any traffic coming from a mile off.

"Styx?"

He was lying down in the backseat. He lifted up his head long enough to grin at us. "Where are you guys off to in such a hurry?"

No words came out of me.

"Uh, to see you," Bobby Gene said. "We thought you were in the hospital."

"Not anymore," Styx said. "They can't keep me down."

"I need to get him home," said the woman behind the wheel. Styx's foster mother, most likely. "You boys should get on home too."

"Come by the house and visit," Styx said. "Don't think I'll be wandering through the woods anytime soon."

Another car approached. The woman looked through the windshield. "Go on and get out of the road," she said. "Get on back home now, you hear?"

"Yes, ma'am," Bobby Gene said.

She flipped the car around and zipped off. Bobby Gene and I picked up our bikes. Our attempted escape—*my* attempted escape—felt stupid now. Even if we'd made it to the hospital, Styx wasn't there to be found. He was being brought back to us, too damaged to complete his own escape.

I laid my head on my handlebars. Who was I kidding? If Styx Malone himself couldn't get out of Sutton on the Grasshopper, what chance did I have on my dirt bike?

The oncoming car slowed. In the bright sunshine, we didn't recognize the vehicle until it got very close.

Uh-oh.

It was Mom.

She braked hard beside us, put on her blinkers and jumped out of the car. "WHAT were you thinking?" she shrieked. "GET in this car, right this minute."

We were in for it now.

Mom made us put our bikes in the back of the station wagon. "And your father will be locking the tires the minute we get home," she told us. "You obviously cannot be trusted with this responsibility any longer. You are out of chances, young men."

"Sorry, Mom." Bobby Gene got in the car.

I stared past Mom's taillights, stared down the road at

whatever was out there. Knowing I'd never see any of it. The world had conspired to keep us in Sutton. We'd be grounded for all eternity, at this rate.

"Caleb," Mom said.

I took one last look, then climbed into the backseat. Slammed the door.

Miracles, my foot.

# CHAPTER 51

## RECKONING

This was sure to be it for us and Styx. We'd broken all the rules. Mom and Dad would never let us hang out with him again. Dad was probably out shopping for chains to lock us to our bedposts.

And maybe it was just as well. Styx Malone already had one foot out the door.

"I called the hospital," Mom announced as we walked into the house. "They sent Styx home this afternoon."

Dad released a satisfied sigh. "See? No cause to go into the city. A little patience was all we needed."

Flames of rage licked down my hard green sides.

I stalked toward our room. Bobby Gene came with me.

"Do I need to nail your window shut?" Dad called after us.

"Bobby, please," Mom said. She followed us down the hall. "Can't you see they're hurting?"

I slammed the door in her face.

Our parents stood outside the door, discussing us. They didn't even bother to tell us we were grounded. We knew.

"I will take them over to Styx's house in the morning," Mom said. "So they can say goodbye."

"Over my dead body," Dad snapped.

"The last time we forbade them, look what happened!" Mom's voice rose. "There is more than one way to take care of this family." She breathed, calming herself.

"No." Dad's voice cut through.

Silence.

Finally Dad said, "I will take them over there right now. This nonsense ends tonight."

✦ ✦ ✦

Mom took the car and headed back to work. Dad followed us through the woods to Styx's house. It was weird, taking Dad along on this path we'd walked dozens of times. I'd never imagined him even approaching the portal that led us into the world we shared with Styx. It no longer felt like a magical journey. Dad was here to put a damper on everything we'd worked for.

We knocked on the porch door.

Styx's foster mother let us in. Dad stayed in the foyer, explaining our situation. We went on into the living room, where Styx was laid out on the couch with a bunch of pillows under him, looking perky as all get-out.

"Well, if it isn't Caleb and B.G." Styx offered his trademark grin.

For once, it wasn't enough. The betrayal cut too deep.

"You were leaving us. How could you do that?"

"Naw, I'd never leave you guys." He smiled. "What are you talking about?"

Bobby Gene brought forward Styx's backpack. He plunked it down at the side of the couch. Evidence. "You were going to take the Grasshopper and go. You never planned to share it with us. You used us."

"You tricked us," I said. "We had the fireworks and you got us to help you."

"We thought you were our friend," Bobby Gene said. "And all you really wanted was a way out of town."

"We cared about you. How could you leave?"

Styx rested for a moment. He didn't try to grease his way out of it. "You don't understand how it is," he said finally.

I crossed my arms. "So tell us."

Styx looked at his hands. "Once they found out about the motor, they weren't going to let me stay. Better to go on my own terms."

"You were leaving before that," I accused him. That morning, before we got the Grasshopper, he'd been sitting on the steps, packing his bag.

Styx's eyes flashed, remembering that morning. "You left me first," he accused us. "Said you couldn't see me anymore. What did it matter if I was here or not?"

Dad came in from the foyer then. "Okay, boys, say goodbye to Styx. We're going home."

"No!" we protested. We weren't done.

"Styx needs to rest," Dad said. "This is not a discussion."

"Don't leave us," Bobby Gene told Styx as he moved toward the door. "We're not finished."

Styx shrugged, then grimaced. "I've got bruised-up ribs and no wheels. Where am I gonna go?"

"See you tomorrow," we said.

"Oh, no," Dad said. "You two are confined to the premises."

"But—"

"Don't argue with me."

We had already pushed our luck as far as we should. But some switch had flipped inside me. I didn't know how to stop.

"Styx is fine," I argued. "What's the big deal?"

"He shouldn't be fine! No one walks away from an accident like that. What if it had been you? Or you?" Dad pulled us close. He clung to us, tearful.

"I guess it coulda gone a different way," Styx said. "But I don't regret taking the ride."

Dad shook his head. "You could have died. I don't know how you got so lucky."

"We all die eventually, Mr. Franklin," Styx said. "I want to have lived."

"You're reckless," Dad said. "I don't want my boys learning that."

"You want us to live in a box?" I said.

"I want you safe. Until you understand what the world is really like, I want you close." He stroked our arms. "I don't want you going somewhere where people might look at you and see a threat. Here, we're just like everybody else."

Styx motioned me closer. He leaned to me and whispered. "You and I've got something in common. We know we're more than what they see."

"They?" But I could feel the truth of it.

"The world," Styx said.

I nodded. How do you move through the world knowing that you're special, when no one else can see it? How do you survive knowing that there's more to you than anyone will ever touch? That you're bigger than your own skin? Bigger, even, than your own room, or house, or town?

Glancing over my shoulder, Styx said, "Or maybe it's not the whole world who needs to know it."

I spun to face Dad.

"You always tell me that I'm just like everyone else!" I cried. "But I'm not. I'm not . . . ordinary."

Dad looked stricken. "Of course you're not ordinary."

"But you always say we are."

"No. It's—I mean—when I say that, I mean we're equal—" Dad sputtered around it. Then he stopped. He suddenly seemed very sad. "Oh, Caleb," he said. And his arms went around me again.

"You want us to be smaller," I whispered. "What if I want to do something big?" *Will you still love me?* I couldn't get those last words out of my mouth.

"Dad." Bobby Gene spoke when I couldn't. "A lot has happened this summer. And we were a little afraid to tell you about any of it."

Dad nodded. "I'm starting to get a sense of that."

Bobby Gene wasn't finished. "We know you love us. We know you want to protect us. But maybe we're ready to see a little bit of the world outside of Sutton."

Bobby Gene met my gaze. Then he reached right across that ocean and took my hand. I wondered if it was hard for him, saying the right thing at the right time to Dad. Sticking up for me, when so much of what we'd done with Styx had pushed him to the limits, and beyond.

I was wrong about my brother. He wasn't on the ordinary side of the canyon with Dad.

He was the bridge.

# CHAPTER 52

## STYX AND STONES

On the third morning we were grounded, Mom said, "Go outside. I can't stand it anymore with you two climbing the walls."

"Outside?" Bobby Gene said tentatively. "You mean, into the backyard?" We didn't want to push our luck.

Mom smiled a little. "You may go into the woods."

We scooted out the door before she could change her mind.

✦ ✦ ✦

Styx looked about as happy to be cooped up as the two of us had. But there was no way to mope in Pixie's presence. She sprinkled fairy dust on the room, literally. For luck.

I supposed it was a bit of luck that she was even here. Her new foster home was not so far away, and the family was nice enough to help her keep in touch. When she'd heard about the accident, she'd come to cheer Styx up. She pirouetted and sparkles rained down.

"That can't be good for our lungs," I commented.

"Hush," she said. She went ahead and glittered up the place. "You may be visited by fairies now," she warned Styx.

"Good fairies, or troublemaking fairies?"

Pixie paused her sprinkling and regarded him seriously. "I can't be sure. They gravitate toward type."

"Then you can be sure," Bobby Gene and I said in unison. Styx laughed. We looked at each other and finished it off. "Troublemaking."

Pixie clapped her hands, delighted. A cloud of sparkles descended.

"Stop making me laugh," Styx said. "It hurts to laugh."

We attempted very solemn expressions.

"Never mind, that's just making it worse," Styx groaned.

"We could take turns insulting you," Pixie suggested.

"Sticks and stones may break my bones," he intoned. "Oh, wait . . ."

Pixie, Bobby Gene and I glanced at each other. We curled in our lips, struggling to stay quiet.

"What?" Styx said. "You didn't ask *me* not to make *you* laugh. It's just me who's on restriction."

We cracked up.

"Penny!" someone called from downstairs. Pixie hugged us all goodbye and twirled her way out of the room.

"That girl"—Bobby Gene shook his head—"is some kind of crazy."

"My kind of crazy, I guess," Styx said. The small smile on his face was different than usual. Calm, as if he understood that when Pixie went away this time, it might not be forever.

"Our kind." Styx was still one of us. We were three parts of a whole. And he needed to be reminded.

There was silence for a moment.

"Why are you here?" Styx asked. "You just got sprung. You've got better things to do than be inside with me."

We didn't, really. "You're our best friend," I said.

"Heck, you're practically part of the family," Bobby Gene argued. "You've eaten Mom's style rice. You'll never be able to leave us now."

Styx closed his eyes. "Man, that rice was good."

"See?" Bobby Gene said.

"We can bring you some style rice," I said.

"Yeah? You think she'd make me some?"

"Sure. You've got the pity angle going," Bobby Gene said. "You could probably get anything you wanted."

"I don't need pity rice," Styx snapped. Then he paused a second and breathed it out. "Naw. I'm gonna save my pity capital for something bigger."

"Like what?" Bobby Gene asked.

"I'm still formulating," Styx said. "It'll be good, though. My body may be a bit dented, but my mind is still sharp."

"Sharp as a tack?" I said.

"Sharp as a shark's tooth," Styx said. "It's like knives up in there."

"Oh, that's a good one," Bobby Gene said. "We have to remember that one." He slapped the doorframe on his way out to the bathroom.

When we were alone, Styx said, "You know what, Caleb?"

"Hmm?"

"We shoulda stopped time on the day we got it."

"The Grasshopper?" Like a waterfall of snapshots, the memories splashed through my mind.

"I waited too long," he said. "I shoulda stopped it after the first ride, before . . . That was stupid. I thought it was gonna go different."

"At Pike's?" I asked.

Styx raised a shoulder. His signature move, still intact. "I woulda told him I was sorry, ya know? And maybe . . ." His voice trailed off.

"He seems like a good guy," I said. "He cares about you a lot."

"Naw. He comes all the way to the ER and doesn't even say hello? Anyway," Styx said. "I thought you'd get what I mean."

"Yeah?"

"We were too busy thinking about what might come next. We missed our happy ending."

"Hey," I said. "It's not the end yet. Nowhere near."

Styx stared at the ceiling. "Anyway. You can tell your dad he doesn't have to worry about me and my bad influence much longer."

I frowned. "What are you talking about?"

Styx raised his shoulder. "They're sending me away again. Soon as I have a clean bill of health."

"Sending you where?"

"Don't know yet. They're running out of places to stick me."

I shook my head. "You can't go."

Styx closed his eyes. "Yeah. We lost the Grasshopper," he said. "Now I'm never gonna be able to go anywhere."

"Maybe you aren't supposed to go. Maybe this is where you belong."

"Nah," he said. "It's just where I'm stuck for a little while longer."

# CHAPTER 53

## A GENEROUS OFFER

We were getting ready for bed. Over the sound of our teeth brushing, I heard Mom say Styx's name. I lowered the flow of my water to a trickle and motioned Bobby Gene to do the same.

"DCS has to find him someplace to go," Mom said. "He's still a kid."

Bobby Gene turned up his water to rinse.

"Shh," I said, slamming his faucet handle down. When I craned my ears again, the moment had passed.

"What are they talking about?" Bobby Gene asked. "I can't hear."

"Styx not having a home to go to," I said. "No one wants him."

"We want him," Bobby Gene said.

"That's right. So let's see what we can do."

We marched straight to our room. It didn't take long to come up with a plan. What took all night was figuring out how to convince Mom and Dad. We needed to make a presentation worthy of Styx.

✦ ✦ ✦

We came down to the breakfast table armed with our plan. We laid it all out on the table, right among the bowls of Wheat Chex and peeled baby oranges.

"What's all this?" Mom was wary.

"We have a presentation," I informed her. "These are our props."

"Okay," Mom said.

"We want to give Styx a home," I announced. And we proceeded to show her our plans.

Mom's eyebrows shot up. "I'm gonna stop you right there. Bobby," she called for Dad.

"Here." Dad ambled into the kitchen. He glanced around at the three of us. "Uh-oh, what'd I do this time?" He grinned.

"Family meeting," Mom announced.

Our parents sat us down. We repeated our pitch to Dad.

"Wow," Dad said. "I mean, that's all very thoughtful, but we can't possibly—"

"Let's talk about this," Mom interrupted. "There are a number of challenges to bringing Styx here. You understand why this is difficult, right?"

I gritted my teeth. It was like they weren't even listening. This was why we did a presentation.

"We don't have a fourth bedroom, for one," Dad pointed out.

"We'll share our room." I shuffled through our sketches to find the place where we'd drawn a loft bed for Bobby Gene over our current dressers. We'd spent a fair amount of our planning time discussing the logistics of possible loft-to-loft sword fights.

Dad jumped in again. "We can't take Styx in. It's a huge responsibility, and very expensive to add another child to the household."

"We thought of that." I handed Dad our money sheet.

"This is all our piggy bank savings," Bobby Gene explained. Some of it actually was leftover Grasshopper cash, but there was no need to point that out.

"And this is a list of chores we can charge people money for. We can raise a hundred dollars per month, we think. Two hundred dollars in the summers."

Our parents stared at us in silence.

"See, we thought of everything," I said.

"You are incredibly generous boys," Dad said. "I—" He cleared his throat. "That's truly extraordinary. I'm so proud of you." He seemed all choked up.

"Extra-ordinary?" I echoed. No. No. No no no no no. Being a good friend was entirely the opposite of ordinary. Styx had showed us that. Why didn't Dad understand?

I took a deep breath and pushed down my feelings. There was a bigger issue now. Dad thought he was paying us a compliment. That was what mattered. "So that means you think it's good, right? You like the idea?"

"I'm afraid it's still a no," Mom said.

I scrambled up from the table. "No! We have to fix it." I turned to Dad. "It's your fault they're sending him away in the first place. You called DCS on him!"

Dad took a deep breath. "You and Bobby Gene are my responsibility. Styx is someone else's. We all care about him, but what he was doing was wrong. And the people responsible for him needed to know about it."

"Styx is our responsibility," I declared. "We're his friends. He doesn't have anyone else."

Mom's expression tightened. "I know, sweetie. I know."

I couldn't hold it in anymore. Not with them looking at us like that and thinking we were useless because we were so young. "We have to help him. His parents died, I think, and his foster mom won't keep him now, and she isn't even the first place he's been. And they took him away from Mr. Pike, who loves him, and now—"

"Mr. Pike?" Mom interjected. "What makes you say they took him away from Mr. Pike?"

I stopped talking, but I couldn't stop my tears. All I wanted was to make a difference for Styx, the way he'd made a difference for us.

Bobby Gene said, "Mr. Pike told us. At the hospital. He said they took Styx away and he never knew why."

"But Styx thinks Mr. Pike didn't want him anymore," I recalled.

Mom closed her eyes. "Let me make a couple of calls," she said. "Sometimes the foster care system gets its signals crossed. But I think we just figured out what's happening here." She came around the table and hugged me and Bobby Gene to her sides.

"My brave and wonderful boys," she said. "Styx is lucky to have good friends like you."

She left the table. So then it was just us and Dad, sitting there. He looked at us. His face said he was thinking about what to say. We waited.

"Go to your room, please," he said. "I'll be right there. I have something I want to show you."

✦ ✦ ✦

Dad showed up in our doorway a few minutes later.

"I just want you to be safe," he said, his voice thick. "You know how much we love you."

We nodded. He had an envelope in his hand.

"Open it," he said.

We did, and found six tickets to the Children's Museum of Indianapolis.

# CHAPTER 54

## ONE EXTRAORDINARY SUMMER

Dad took all of us kids to the museum the week before school started. Me, Bobby Gene, Styx and even Cory Cormier. Pixie met us there.

It was the best day of our lives. We saw all the fossils. We saw the dinosaur climbing up the side of the building. We rode the giant merry-go-round. We went from top to bottom a couple of times, making sure we saw everything.

On the ride home, Dad informed us that Mom had a special surprise guest waiting for us.

We dropped off Cory first, then went to Styx's place. Mr. Pike's truck was parked in the driveway.

Styx perked up in his seat, then slouched back down. "Why's he here?"

Dad smiled across the console at him. "Why do you think?"

"For real?" Styx sounded skeptical.

Dad nodded. "Only if you want it."

Styx was the first one out of the car. He bounded into the house. We were right on his heels.

"Yes!" he shouted. He didn't even stop to greet Mr. Pike. Ran straight past him and up to his bedroom.

"Mr. Pike!" We waved. He was standing by the front door.

"You're here to visit?" I said, even though my heart had started to tick faster. A tiny hope sprouted.

Mr. Pike stepped forward. He had his hat in his hand, slapping it against his leg. Today he looked a trifle nervous.

"I'm here to visit, yeah," he said. "And . . . to ask Styx if he wants to come home."

Bobby Gene and I bumped shoulders in excitement. If we couldn't take Styx home, this was the next best thing. "Really?" we asked. "For keeps?"

Mr. Pike nodded. "I'd like him to be my boy, if he'll have me."

✦ ✦ ✦

We followed Styx up to his bedroom. Supposedly to help him pack, but he popped his clothes into the backpack and he was ready to go.

He turned to us with a whole new kind of smile. Half happy, half sad, but content all the way around.

Oh. Styx's happy ending was going to take him away from us. We wouldn't be across-the-woods neighbors anymore.

"Hey, guys?" he said. "Thanks."

We hugged him.

"That was the best summer ever," Styx said. "Truly extraordinary."

"Totally," I echoed.

"Extra-ordinary," Bobby Gene chimed in, pumping his fist.

*No, no, no.* My head spun. Not extra-ordinary . . .

"Completely off the hook." Styx grinned as he slapped us five, one with each hand.

My hand moved automatically . . . even as my brain clanged like a bell, connecting the dots. *Extraordinary.* Styx knew that guys like him and me . . . we were something more.

Oh, no. I slapped my palm against my forehead.

*Extra-ordinary.* Bobby Gene pronounced it like Dad did. As if it was two words. But it wasn't. It was the same word.

I busted out laughing. What a silly mistake!

Styx and Bobby Gene stared at me, as if to say "What?"

"Extraordinary," I choked out.

If only I'd realized what it meant in the first place, when the word slipped out of Dad's mouth on the third of July, before I went and got us in a whole mess of trouble.

But . . . sometimes trouble is underrated.

✦ ✦ ✦

We trooped down the stairs and watched as Styx drove away with Mr. Pike in his truck. Styx made a crazy face at us through the window. We made crazy faces back, then shook our heads and smiled. Mr. Pike was going to have his hands full.

Bobby Gene linked his arm through mine. We squeezed our elbows together as we walked to the car. It would be just us again. But things were different now.

At first it seemed like Styx Malone had everything to teach us, but it turned out he had plenty to learn. About how special he was and how much he changed us. He might have saved us from a heck of a boring summer, but really, we ended up saving him, too.

When the train whistle blows—the one coming in or the one going out—I think of him.

No one would ever call Styx Malone ordinary.

Turns out, no one would ever call Caleb Franklin ordinary either. Not even Dad.

✦ ✦ ✦

We hung the Grasshopper piece on the wall of our bedroom. MIRACLES. A reminder of the way Styx Malone defied death.

Styx defied all the odds, of course. He got adopted at

sixteen. He got a job and started saving for a new set of wheels. He had himself a couple of lifelong friends, and we never let him forget it. He kept his eye on the horizon, because that's who he is, but he stopped trying to run.

Styx laughed the first time he saw our odd little Grasshopper monument. "There's no such thing as miracles."

Bobby Gene and I only smiled. Styx Malone wasn't right about everything, it turned out.

Every night, before I fall asleep, I touch the pictures hanging on my ceiling. I'm in some of them now. There's one of us all at the museum. I've also got train stubs from the time Dad took us to Chicago, and a picture of us on the shore of Lake Michigan, with the waves lapping at our feet.

I touch each one, like a ritual. Then I look at the Grasshopper piece, remembering how Styx Malone shook up our world, and how he finally got his happy ending.

And how we got ours, too.

Were there more happy endings in our future? Who knew? None of us were done living yet.

# ACKNOWLEDGMENTS

I remain deeply grateful to my family and the many friends who support, uplift, comfort, and inspire me as I work. Special thanks to Will Alexander for his early manuscript notes, and to his entire family for keeping me company and making sure I ate meals when the deadlines were looming. Also thanks to Nicole Valentine, Emily Kokie, Sarah Badavas, Cynthia Leitich Smith, David Gill, Nova Ren Suma, Tirzah Price, Alice Dodge, Grace Lester, Andrea T., and Kerry Land for their support, as well as all my colleagues at Vermont College of Fine Arts. I very much enjoyed my time with the staff at the Children's Museum of Indianapolis, who talked to me about fossils! Thanks to my agent, Ginger Knowlton, and her team at Curtis Brown, Ltd., for their work in bringing my work to the world. Finally, thanks to my editor, Wendy Lamb, along with Dana Carey and all the people at Random House who have combined their creative talents to transform this book from an idea to a reality.